Tiger in Trouble

Tiger in Trouble

Eric Walters

An imprint of
Beach Holme Publishing
Vancouver

First Edition

This book is published by Beach Holme Publishing, 226–2040 West 12th Avenue, Vancouver, B.C. V6J 2G2. *www.beachholme.bc.ca*. This is a Sandcastle Book.

The publisher gratefully acknowledges the financial support of the Canada Council for the Arts and of the British Columbia Arts Council. The publisher also acknowledges the financial assistance received from the Government of Canada through the Book Publishing Industry Development Program (BPIDP) for its publishing activities.

The Canada Council | Le Conseil des Arts
for the Arts | du Canada

BRITISH
COLUMBIA
ARTS COUNCIL

Editor: Jen Hamilton
Production and Design: Jen Hamilton
Cover Art: Ron Lightburn
Author Photograph: Paula Esplen

Printed and bound in Canada by Marc Veilleux Imprimeur

National Library of Canada Cataloguing in Publication Data

Walters, Eric, 1957-
 Tiger in trouble

"A Sandcastle book."
ISBN 0-88878-420-1

I. Title.
PS8595.A598T53 2001   jC813'.54   C2001-910125-2
PZ7.W17129Ti 2001

For my youngest daughter, Julia,
who said there needed to be a sequel

Acknowledgements

I'd like to thank Peter Klose and the staff of Jungle Cat World for letting me spend time at their wonderful wildlife park in Orono, Ontario.

And I'd like to acknowledge Werner Ebner, a gentleman who has room in his heart for all the tigers, lions, cougars, and assorted other animals who live in his backyard. Special thanks to you and your dedicated volunteers at Bear Creek Exotic Animal Sanctuary who have all shared your time, expertise, and passion.

Chapter 1

"I don't understand why we have to go," I said to Mr. McCurdy as we left his house and stolled toward the barn.

"It's only going to be for a week, Sarah," he answered.

"That's one week too long. All I wanted to do this summer was to hang around, spend time with my friends, and help you with your animals."

"I think I can take care of the animals for a few days without your help. And it's not like I don't have help besides the two of you."

He was right about that. All of our friends were always over to help.

"I've got so many people helping that I could go away for a few days, so I think we can get by without you and your brother for a week. It isn't like you're being sent to jail. You're going to a camp."

"A camp," I muttered, shaking my head. "I'm way too old to be going to any stupid camp!"

Mr. McCurdy laughed. "Sarah, unless my memory is failing...and it does happen when you get to be seventy-five, you're only fourteen. As far as I can tell, about the only things you're too old for are diapers, soothers, and tricycles!"

"Funny, very funny."

"I try. Besides, it might even be fun," Mr. McCurdy said.

"Don't you remember that my brother is coming with me?

How could anything involving Nick be fun?"

"I don't know why you'd say something like that. Nick always seems like a real hoot to me."

"He's a real *something*," I said under my breath.

"And it sounds like it's going to be exciting. Just imagine, an exotic animal camp. What did you say they called it?"

"Zoo camp. I guess it could be...okay," I admitted reluctantly.

"When I was your age, the only way I could learn about animals was to run away and join the carnival. Who knows, you might learn some things about animals."

"I already know lots about animals, and anything I don't know I can learn right here from you!" I protested.

"That's a mighty fine compliment, Sarah, but there's lots of things that a broken-down old carnival man like me doesn't know that you might learn at that camp. I bet they have some mighty fine experts there."

"First off, you're not broken-down, and second, I bet you know more about animals than most of the experts in the whole world!"

Mr. McCurdy smiled. "Well, I do know a thing or two about animals and..." He paused. "I noticed you didn't argue the part about me being old."

"Um...it was just...that—"

Mr. McCurdy started to laugh again. "Don't go twisting yourself into a pretzel there, girl. I was just funning with ya! Who could argue with me being old? I think the only thing around this farm that's older than me is the dirt under my feet. Here," he said as he handed me the feed bucket, "I'm going to see if I can find Brent while you feed Buddha."

I took the bucket from him. It held two dead chickens, their heads hanging over the side of the pail. As I walked across the barn floor, Buddha got to his feet and came toward the bars of his cage. Even though I'd known Buddha for almost a year, even though I knew he was safely in the cage and couldn't get out, even though I knew he liked me and wouldn't hurt me, the sight of him standing there still took my breath away. Something about an eight-hundred-pound Siberian tiger gliding across the floor, his golden eyes glowing brightly, made the hairs on the back of my neck and arms stand right up.

"How are you doing, boy?" I asked softly as I stopped at the cage.

He rubbed his head against the bars, causing them to surge out slightly under his weight. Hesitantly and slowly I reached a hand between the bars and scratched Buddha behind one of his ears. He loved being rubbed there, and he pressed hard against my hand.

Suddenly he spun his head around and his tongue flicked out and licked my fingers. Instantly I withdrew my hand. I knew Buddha wouldn't hurt me—at least he hadn't in the ten months I'd known him—but I still didn't like any part of me near that massive mouth.

With one hand I pulled a dead chicken out of the bucket and tried to hide it behind my back so Buddha couldn't see it. Then I took the bucket and set it on the ground with a noisy thud. Buddha stared at the bucket that he knew always contained food. I'd placed it clearly in his view, but far enough away from the bars so he couldn't reach out a paw and hook it toward him.

Casually, while Buddha focused on the feed bucket, I moved to the far end of the cage. Slowly I reached between the bars, swung the chicken, and tossed it into the cage. As it flew, its legs, wings, and head pinwheeled out, and then Buddha bounded across the pen and grabbed it mid-flight! There was a sickening sound as his jaws clamped shut with a snap. Most of the chicken had disappeared, locked away inside his mouth with only the legs and one wing hanging outside. I didn't know what amazed me more: how big Buddha was, or how something that big could possibly be that quick and coordinated.

I leaned against the bars and watched with fascination as Buddha spit out the bird and grabbed it between his front paws.

Carefully, almost delicately, he began to "pluck" the chicken, pulling out the feathers with his teeth and spitting them on the ground. Mr. McCurdy said that some tigers just ate birds feathers and all, but some cats were like Buddha 'and were more particular.

I guess being around Buddha, and all of Mr. McCurdy's animals, was one of the reasons I thought it was strange to go to this camp we were being sent to. Most kids would think it was really something to go to an exotic animal camp, but for me and my brother all we had to do was cross a couple of fields from our farm to the neighbouring farm and there we were with Mr. McCurdy and his animals. There was a time last year when the old mayor and some of the other politicians had tried to make Mr. McCurdy give up his animals. They thought it was dangerous to have exotic animals around. With my mother's help he was able to keep all of them. As long as he took good care of them, he could have whatever he wanted on his farm.

"Can't find that darn snake anywhere," Mr. McCurdy said as he came up beside me. "Maybe you and Nick can help me find him before you go home today."

"Maybe Nick can," I said. "But not me."

"I don't know why you don't like my snake."

"It's not just your snake I don't like," I said. "I don't like anybody's snake."

"But Brent's a good snake." Brent was Mr. McCurdy's ten-foot-long Burmese Python.

"As far as I'm concerned, the words *good* and *snake* do not ever belong in the same sentence," I said.

"Don't go saying things like that," Mr. McCurdy said. "Brent might overhear you and get his feelings hurt. He's a pretty sensitive snake."

"His feelings are the last thing in the world I'm worried about hurting," I grumbled.

Of course, I didn't know exactly where Brent was, but I did

know he was somewhere in the barn. He had the run of the whole building: bedding down under the straw, moving through the stalls, hunting down any mice or any rats unfortunate enough to take up residence in the barn. It was eerie to be walking through the barn and catch a glimpse of Brent moving across the floor. Or even worse, to see him hanging from the beams or pipes above your head. I quickly glanced up at the ceiling. There was no snake above me right now—thank goodness!

"Are there any snakes at that zoo camp you're going to?" Mr. McCurdy asked.

"I don't know, but I certainly hope not."

"You've really got to try and get over your fear of snakes. If you'd ever spent any time around Brent, you'd learn he's just an old cuddly python."

I couldn't help but shudder. I knew how pythons "cuddled" with people, and it was a lot more than simply a hug.

Mr. McCurdy reached down and grabbed the second chicken from the feed bucket. "You weren't planning on saving this one for my dinner, were you?" he asked as he held it up.

"I was hoping you'd be having dinner with us tonight," I said.

"Nope, not tonight. When you get back, I'll come over. Do you want me to save this chicken until then?" he asked, waving the dead bird in my face.

"I only want my chicken as McNuggets...along with large fries and a Coke."

Mr. McCurdy chuckled loudly. "Thank goodness old Buddha here isn't quite as particular as you."

He thrust the bird between the bars and tossed it toward the tiger. Without even standing up Buddha flicked out a paw and deflected the flying fowl, causing it to fall right beside the remains of the first chicken.

"Let's get back up to the house. You and Nick have to be home soon, don't you?"

I looked at my watch. It was almost five o'clock, and I'd

promised my mom that we'd be back by six when she returned from work. She was bringing home supper. With my luck it would be chicken. I was hoping for pizza.

"Are you sure you don't want to join us for supper?"

"As sure as I was when you asked me thirty seconds ago, and twenty minutes ago, and an hour ago, and first thing this morning and—"

"Okay, I get it."

"Good!"

I'd tried a number of times to convince Mr. McCurdy to join us for supper tonight. It wasn't unusual for him to eat at our house—he did it a couple of times a week—but he kept saying no this time. He said he thought it should just be "family" at my house tonight because it was the last dinner we'd have together before Nick and I went away for camp.

Of course, Mr. McCurdy wasn't family, but he was more than just a neighbour or a friend. He was sort of like a grandfather. I mean, what I thought a grandfather would be. One of mine had died long before I was born, and the other passed on when I was only three, so I didn't even have any memories of him.

Actually, I only knew one grandparent. That was my mother's mother, my Nana, and really, I hadn't known her that well, either. It was strange, but when she was alive and living halfway across the country, we'd only see her a couple of times a year at holidays or special occasions like weddings or funerals. Then she died, at the same time as my parents separated, and our mother brought us here to live...leaving behind our home and lives and friends to move into the same farmhouse that my mother had grown up in.

It was hard to believe we'd been here less than a year. The only thing harder to believe was how angry I'd been about the move. I'd been so mad at our mother for tearing us away from everything and dragging us thousands of kilometres away from our lives. I'd been even more angry at her than I'd been at my father for leaving us. But now? This was my home.

Mr. McCurdy pulled open the door of the house and we walked in. I trailed behind him down the hall and into the kitchen.

"Is there a winner yet?" Mr. McCurdy asked.

"Not yet, but he's cracking," my brother said.

He was sitting on a chair on one side of the kitchen table. Sitting on the opposite side was Calvin, Mr. McCurdy's chimpanzee. The big ape had his arms propped on the table and his head resting on his hands. His eyes were wide open. The two of them were having a staring contest.

Of course, only Nick really knew they were having a contest— at least I thought only Nick knew. Sometimes you couldn't tell what that chimp knew and didn't know. If nothing else, the ape *was* as smart as Nick, so I guess that made this an even contest.

"How long are you going to keep this up?" I asked.

"As long as it takes," Nick replied.

I laughed. "Stupid ape."

"Calvin's not stupid!" Nick protested.

"I wasn't talking about Calvin."

"Funny, Sarah, really funny."

I walked across the room and took a seat at the edge of the couch. The rest of the couch was taken up by Laura, Mr. McCurdy's cheetah. She opened one eye, lifted her head, and then plopped it back on top of my leg, closing her eyes again. I rubbed her behind one ear, and she snuggled her head against me. I'd come to love this old cat.

Of course, I'd never do this with Buddha. Cheetahs weren't like tigers, or any other of the big cats. Cheetahs you can trust. Tigers you can only trust a little, and only if you never turn your back on them. Mr. McCurdy had told me about the one time when he was young that he turned his back on a tiger. He said that the claws went *through* his jacket, *through* his shirt, and *into* his back. Mr. McCurdy said if you were smart you only had to make that mistake once, and if you were smarter you never had to make it at all. I aimed for smarter.

I looked over at my brother, staring at the ape, staring at him. "This can't go on much longer, Nick. We have to go home for supper."

"You can leave without me. I don't quit until the chimp quits."

"Maybe rather than outstare him, you should outthink him," Mr. McCurdy said.

"Which one of them are you talking to?" I asked.

"Mainly your brother. Nick, ya gotta distract him."

"How do you suggest I do that?" my brother asked.

"Easy," Mr. McCurdy said. He strolled across the kitchen and opened the fridge. "Anybody want a Coke?" he asked, holding up a can of pop.

Calvin jumped up from his chair and hobbled across the room, taking the Coke from Mr. McCurdy. He popped the top and the can sang out a big *pppppffftttt*.

"There you go," Mr. McCurdy said. "This way you both got something you wanted."

"I'd rather have had the Coke," Nick said.

Calvin extended his arm, offering Nick the pop.

"I think I'll pass. Anyway, what I *really* want is not to have to go away tomorrow," Nick said.

"I don't understand what you two have against going away on a vacation," Mr. McCurdy said.

"I just want to stay here."

"I hope your mamma doesn't know how you feel."

"Well..." I said.

"I think she sort of knows," Nick agreed.

"Too bad. If you stop complaining, at least one person can enjoy your being away at camp."

"Who?" I asked.

"Your mother."

"Our mother?" Nick and I said in unison.

"Of course. She'll have a well-deserved break."

"A break from what?" I questioned.

"You two."

"She doesn't want to get away from us. She said she'd miss us—that she didn't even want us to go," I stated.

"I'm sure she'll miss you," Mr. McCurdy agreed. "But that doesn't mean she won't enjoy a little bit of peace and quiet."

"We're not that bad," I said. "Well, at least *I'm* not that bad."

Nick shot me a dirty look.

"Bad hasn't got anything to do with it," Mr. McCurdy said. "It's just that it can't be easy being a mother and a father to you two. When was the last time she had time away from the both of you?"

"She has time away. She goes out with her friends," I said.

"And on dates, too, sometimes," Nick added.

"That's not what I mean. I bet she hasn't had a night to herself since the three of you moved out here."

"It's a lot longer than that," I said.

"How much longer?"

"Like forever. Since the time I was born."

"Sounds like she should get a little time off every fourteen or so years, don't you think?" Mr. McCurdy asked.

I suddenly felt bad.

"But if she needed some time away, why didn't she arrange it herself?" Nick asked.

The week at camp had been arranged and paid for by our father and given to us as an "end of the school year" graduation present. If he really wanted to give us something, he should have come out here and visited us, or arranged for us to come out to see him. It had been over six months since we'd laid eyes on him, and that was only for a few hours as he was passing through town.

"My guess is that she doesn't even know herself that she needs some time away," he explained. "And even if she did, she'd feel too guilty to arrange it."

"Guilty?" Nick asked. "Why would she feel guilty? I think we should just tell her we don't want to go."

"No, Mr. McCurdy's right," I said. "She does need some time to herself. Whether we like it or not, we're going away to camp, and we're not going to complain about it anymore. Who knows?" I said with a shrug. "Maybe we'll even have a good time."

"I'm really going to miss you two," my mother said.

Nick gave me an "I told you so" look. I tried to ignore him.

"We'll miss you, too," I said. "Could you pass me the fried rice?"

My mother picked up one of the half-dozen little cardboard cartons that sat beside her—the Chinese food she'd brought home for supper—and passed it to me.

"You certainly brought home a lot of food," I said.

"I ordered a meal for four. I was hoping Angus would be joining us tonight."

"I tried to convince him to come," I said.

"I guess it won't just be the two of you, but Angus I'll be missing for the next week."

"You can always invite him over," I suggested. "I know he'd like that."

"I don't think that would work," she said. "I was thinking it would be pretty lonely around here with you two gone."

"That's even more reason to invite Mr. McCurdy over."

"Well..." my mother said. "I really wasn't planning on spending any time around the house, either."

"You can't just work the whole time we're gone. You spend too much time at the office already!" I protested.

"That isn't what I mean. I guess this is the perfect time to tell you something—a surprise."

"What sort of a surprise?" I asked anxiously. I stopped liking surprises when they started becoming things like "your father and I are separating" or "we're moving."

"I was thinking that since the two of you were going to be gone, anyway, that maybe I should take a trip, too."

"You're going away?" Nick asked. He sounded as if he couldn't believe his ears.

"Yes, I'm very excited!"

"Where are you going?" I asked.

"I'm going to the Bahamas."

"The Bahamas?" I gasped.

"I'll be leaving tomorrow. I'll be flying off in one direction while you two are flying off in the other. Isn't that exciting?"

"Yeah...really exciting," I mumbled, too stunned by the news to know what else to say.

"I'm going to a resort on a tiny little island. It's advertised as an escape island."

"What does that mean?" I asked, thinking maybe it was like Mr. McCurdy had said and she was escaping from us.

"It means it's very isolated. You can only get there by boat, and it's very rugged. For example, there's no televisions, radios, computers, Internet, or even telephones!"

I thought she could probably get the same effect if she lived in our barn for the next week.

"Why would anybody want to go someplace that had none of those things?" Nick questioned.

"There'll be other things, like clear skies, warm weather, tropical fruit, and a warm blue ocean!"

I guess the barn didn't have those things going for it.

"But who are you going with?" Nick asked.

"I'm going by myself. Do you know how long it's been since I had time to myself?"

I had a pretty good idea it was at least fourteen years, but I didn't answer.

"It was before I met your father, my second year of university.

Since then I've always had somebody to care for, or look out for, or take their feelings into account. This time I'm going just for me and doing what I want."

I couldn't remember the last time I'd seen her this excited.

"So, while the two of you are having a wonderful adventure, I'm going to be having one of my own!"

"But what if something happens?" Nick asked.

She reached over and put her hand on top of his. "That's so sweet, Nicky, but nothing's going to happen to me. There's a hospital on the main island and—"

·"I mean to us!" he said. "If there's no phone, how can we get in touch with you if something happens to us? It isn't like we can get hold of Dad!"

Mom scowled. It was that look she almost always had when Dad was mentioned. Of course we couldn't get in touch with him, because his whereabouts kept changing. Ever since he left us he'd been living out of suitcases, travelling across the country and around the world. He'd always wanted to be a photographer instead of a businessman, and for the past year that's what he'd been doing.

"You'll be fine," Mom said reassuringly. "If you really need to get me, they can always send a boat over from the big island. I'll give you a number to reach me that way. I've already spoken to your Aunt Ellen, and she's agreed to be your emergency contact. There's nothing to worry about."

I wanted to say something, ask something, comment, question, protest, or complain but, of course, there was nothing I could or should say.

"That's great," I finally mumbled, trying my best to sound enthusiastic.

"How long have you known about this trip?" Nick asked. That was a good question, something that I'd wondered about, too.

"I've been thinking about it for a few days, but it didn't all fall into place until this morning. I guess I could have called, but I wanted to tell you in person."

I believed what she was saying, but it still felt as if this had all been sprung on us, that she sort of snuck up with this plan so we wouldn't have a chance to protest. But really, what right did we have to protest? She deserved a break, too.

"I think that right after supper we should clean up the kitchen, pack our bags, and get a good night's sleep," my mother suggested. "We have to be up very early tomorrow to get to the airport, and I think I'm so excited that I'm going to have a lot of trouble getting to sleep tonight."

I couldn't argue with what she was saying. I knew I'd have a whole lot of difficulty getting to sleep myself. Excitement had nothing to do with it in my case, though.

"Since I made supper, you two should clean up the kitchen," Mom said.

"Made supper!" Nick protested. "You only carried it through the door!"

"Yes, but I made the money that bought the supper," she said with a laugh. "Besides, while you're cleaning up I'll go down to the basement and get out our luggage...unless one of you two would like to do that?"

"Not me!" I cried, holding up my hands. "The kitchen sounds just fine to me. Come on, Nick, give me a hand."

He got up from his chair. "Okay, what do you want me to do?"

I shook my head. "Figure it out, Nick. This isn't brain surgery. Start off by closing the little cartons. We'll bring them over to Mr. McCurdy tonight."

"We will?"

"There's no point in leaving leftover Chinese food here for a week. It'll be bad before we get back," I explained. "I guess he was wrong...he will end up sharing our supper."

"I think that's the only thing he was wrong about," Nick said as he started doing what I'd told him. "It sounds like Mom isn't going to miss us that much."

"Everybody needs a break, and we'll be back soon enough," I offered as I put the plates into the soap-filled sink.

"I just hope it'll be soon enough."

"What do you mean by that?"

"I mean it's hard to be away from people for that long...I just hope they don't change the way they feel, that's all."

"Nick, you are totally insane! We're only going away for a week, and Mom will still feel exactly the same way about us!"

"I wasn't talking about Mom," he said softly.

"Then who?"

"My friends."

"Your friends?"

Nick suddenly turned red and looked at the ground. "My girlfriend."

"Girlfriend? What are you talking about?"

"I sort of have a girlfriend." He turned redder with each word.

"You do?"

"Yeah. Her name is Tori. You've even spoken to her on the phone."

"You have lots of friends who call."

"She's the only girl who calls."

"I've got news for you, Nick. Half your friends sound like girls."

"They do not!"

"Almost all eleven-year-old boys sound like eleven-year-old girls. Besides, what exactly does, 'having a girlfriend' mean?" I questioned.

"It means that she likes me and I like her, and that sometimes we go places with each other, or eat lunch at the same table at school, or talk on the phone."

"That sounds like things I do with my friends who are boys, but that doesn't make any of them my boyfriend."

"Of course not," Nick said. "That would involve somebody wanting to have you as a girlfriend, and that's a long shot...unless maybe the boy was blind, or stupid, or desperate, or maybe he was feeling sorry for you, or he lost a bet or—"

"Are you two fighting again!" Mom asked as she came back into the kitchen carrying two suitcases.

"I'm not fighting!" I protested.

"Good. That's not how we should be spending our last night together."

"Aren't you forgetting something?" Nick said. "This is only the last night the three of us are spending together. Sarah and I are going away together."

That was just like Nick: always finding a way to make a bad situation even more irritating for me. I didn't know who this Tori girl was, but she must be really, really tolerant.

❧

Some people counted sheep. Others counted their blessings. I had even heard of people who counted the number of little holes in the ceiling tiles over their beds. Me, I counted things I was worried about.

We were going away to a place I didn't know. My mother was going away to another place I didn't know. My brother was going with me, so that meant I was in charge of him. My brother didn't like my being in charge of him. He was always looking for ways to get into trouble and was good at finding those ways. We were all going away in airplanes. Two airplanes, which meant there were twice as many chances that one of them might crash. Sure, they say airplanes are safer than cars, but if a car's engine dies, all that happens is that it slows to a stop. It doesn't plunge from the sky and explode. Or for that matter it doesn't crash into the side of a mountain or drop into the ocean—were the Bahamas inside the Bermuda Triangle?

Satisfied that I'd pretty well listed all available problems, I decided it was time to get to sleep. I wondered how many holes *were* in the ceiling tiles over my bed.

Chapter 2

"Okay, is everything turned off?" my mother asked, talking more to herself than to me as she started to check things for the third time.

There is absolutely no question where I got my paranoid side from. She scurried around the house, unplugging electrical appliances, jiggling the handles of the toilets to make sure they wouldn't run over, and checking to see that all the windows were closed and locked.

"Everything's fine," I said reassuringly as she made another pass through the kitchen.

"I just want to make sure. It would be awful if something happened to the house while we were away, and we're going to be gone for a whole week."

"But it isn't as if the house is going to be abandoned," I pointed out. "Mr. McCurdy said he'd come by every day and check on things."

We'd driven over to his place last night right after we'd cleaned up the kitchen to drop off the leftover Chinese food. As soon as he found out that my mother was going away, too, he offered to watch the house.

Actually that was the second thing he did after hearing her news. The first thing was to shoot me a smug little smile that said, "Told ya!" His being right didn't surprise me, because he usually was.

Mr. McCurdy was smart, maybe the smartest person I knew, including my mother. And it wasn't that she wasn't smart—she'd been to university, was a lawyer, and dealt with pretty complex issues in court—it was just that he was smart in a different sort of way. He was, well, I don't know...wise. He reminded me of those old guys in cartoons who sit on the tops of mountains and then people climb all the way up to ask them the meaning of life. I'd never asked him that question, but if I did, I was pretty sure he'd have an answer.

I once told him I thought he was pretty smart. After he stopped laughing, he asked me how anybody who'd only been to high school a couple of years could possibly be smart. He said I was confusing smart with old, and that you couldn't help but learn a thing or two as you got older. It was, he said, just like walking across a really muddy field—the farther you walk the more mud flies up and sticks to you. I knew it was more than that. Lots of people grow older without ever getting any smarter. Heck, there were some people, like my father, who managed to grow older without even growing up.

I made a mental note. That might be something else I'd say to my father when I saw him again. Of course, there was no telling when that might be. At least he was writing us more regularly now, and he did give us this trip...although I didn't know if that was such a good thing.

"That's it," my mom said. "Everything's okay. We have to get going. Where's your brother?"

"He's in the living room on the phone."

"Again? Who's he talking to now?"

"Probably his girlfriend."

"His what? No wait," she said, holding her arms up in surrender. "I don't want to hear about it...not now...and maybe not later. Nick! Get off the phone! We have to get going!"

"I'm off," Nick called out as he pushed through the door and into the kitchen.

"Good. Then get your bags and get out to the car."

"My bags are already out there. I was ready a long time ago. I was just waiting for you two to be ready."

I looked at my mother. "Are you sure you don't want to take him with you?"

She smiled. "Thanks for the offer, dear, but I think he belongs with you. Now we better get going or we'll miss our flights, and then we'll both have him for the week."

I picked up my two bags—a little carryon and a big piece of luggage that contained everything I'd need for the next seven days. Then I pushed open the door, walked out and propped it open with my leg to allow my mother to get out, and...where had she gone to?

"Mom?"

"Coming!" she called, hurrying through the kitchen and clutching her two bags. "I just had to check to make sure the curling iron was unplugged."

I almost laughed. She always had to go back and check on that iron. It got to the point were my father had once packed it in the trunk of the car without telling her. Half a block from home, when she said she needed us to turn around to check it, he simply pulled over to the side of the road, opened the trunk, and pulled it out. My brother, my father, and I all thought it was hilarious. But she didn't think it was that funny.

Nick was already at the car, sitting on the hood, his bags by the trunk. We hurried over to him.

"I'll just pop the trunk, we'll put the bags in, and—" My mother stopped mid-sentence at the sound of a car coming up our driveway. It was Mr. McCurdy driving his big old Cadillac convertible with the top down. Sitting in the back, leaning over the seat, and peering through the windshield was Calvin, who loved a car ride. Mr. McCurdy skidded the car to a stop in front of us, and a plume of dirt and dust blew over and past us.

"I was hoping I wasn't too late!" he called out.

"We should already be gone, but we got distracted checking on things," my mother said. "It was sweet of you to come and say goodbye."

"I didn't come to say goodbye. I came to give the three of you a ride to the airport."

"You don't have to do that," Mom said.

"Of course I don't have to do it, but I want to. It'll cost a fortune to leave your car in the parking lot for a week, and money doesn't grow on trees...at least no trees I've ever seen."

"It's a long way to go, and I don't want to put you out."

"It's not that far, and certainly not far to travel to do a neighbour a favour."

"But if I don't bring my car, how will we get home from the airport at the end of our trip?" Mom asked.

"You'll get back the same way you got there. Just write down your flight information, and I'll be waiting there when you get back."

"That's so nice of you," Mom said.

"But first things first. When do your flights leave?"

"Mine's at ten thirty-five, and the kids catch a flight at eleven," Mom said.

"Well, then, that settles it. I'll drive you all there, put you on your plane, and stay with the kids to make sure they get on their flight safe and sound."

"I'll make sure they're all checked in for their flight," my mother said. "They'll be fine."

"I'm sure they will be, too, but won't your flight be a whole lot easier if you know they're being watched until they get on their flight?" Mr. McCurdy asked.

"Well...I really don't want to put you to all that effort and—"

"Neighbours and family do stuff like this. Besides, if we stand here arguing much longer, you'll all miss your flights. Now throw your luggage in my trunk and let's get going!"

"Please, Mom," Nick pleaded.

"Mr. McCurdy's a great driver," I added.

"Sure, why not!" she said. "But are you certain we can fit all our luggage in your car?"

Mr. McCurdy chuckled. "You could put your whole *car* in my trunk. I know for a fact there's space in there for at least eight hundred pounds of luggage!"

Nick and I exchanged smiles. We knew exactly what he meant. The trunk of his car had been converted into a sort of mobile animal cage. He could put Buddha in there when he needed to move him from one place to another. There was even a special section between the back seats that popped out to allow fresh air and light in.

"Nick, get your mother's bags!" Mr. McCurdy ordered, and Nick grabbed her luggage. Then we brought our bags over and put them in the trunk.

"Can I ride in the back?" Nick asked.

"Where else did you think you were going to ride?" I asked.

"No, I don't mean in the back seat. I mean in the trunk!"

"Luggage in the trunk, people in the seats," Mom answered as she climbed into the front.

I opened one of the back doors to take a spot beside Calvin. Nick slammed the trunk closed with a thud, then leaped in over the door on the other side. He practically landed on top of Calvin, who jumped over and into me.

"Calvin!" I exclaimed.

The chimp shuffled slightly over, blew me a kiss, then reached out and patted me on the head. I guess it could have been worse—sometimes he didn't blow me a kiss but planted a wet one on my cheek.

We started forward, and instinctively I reached down to try to put on my seat belt before I remembered that this car didn't have any. It was so old that it was made before cars even had seat belts. We bumped down our driveway and then stopped at the road. Mr. McCurdy scanned the road in both directions. I was relieved to see he was wearing his special driving glasses. They were a pair of lady's cat's-eye glasses covered in rhinestones. Of course, as long as he could see well when he was wearing them, it didn't matter if they looked silly, .

The way was clear, and he turned onto the road, then quickly picked up speed. The wind whistled over the top of the windshield and blew my hair back. There was no way to keep your hair from becoming a total mess in a convertible. It was probably the most impractical car in the world, which made it hard to explain why I liked driving in it so much.

The only person who seemed to enjoy it as much as I did was Calvin. Well, I guess you could call him a person. He loved nothing better than going for a car ride. Mr. McCurdy always made him sit in the back, and Calvin would prop himself up, lean against the front seat, and stare through the windshield. The only thing funnier than watching Calvin checking out the world as we drove was watching people checking him out. I understood people's reactions—it wasn't every day you saw a chimp in a convertible— but I swear there were times when it seemed as if people were going to run themselves right off the road. I leaned back and decided to enjoy the drive.

In what seemed like a flash, we pulled into the airport parking lot and came to a stop. Mr. McCurdy drove a lot faster than my mother did, and we still had plenty of time to get checked in and onto our flights.

"Thank you so much for the ride," my mother said as we started to pull the luggage out of the trunk. "But what about Calvin? I don't think they'll let him into the airport."

"What if you claimed he was your seeing-eye monkey?" Nick asked.

"Hey, that just might work—nah, we better not," Mr. McCurdy said with a chuckle. "He'll wait out here in the car."

"Is that safe?" my mother asked.

"Sure, he'll probably just lie down and have a little nap. Besides, if he waits here I can be darn sure nobody's going to mess with my car. This thing's a classic, you know."

"But aren't you worried somebody might bother or hurt Calvin?" Mom asked.

"Calvin?" all three of us said at once.

"I can't even think of anything strong enough, or stupid enough, to bother Calvin," Mr. McCurdy said. "He'll be fine. I figure anybody dumb enough to tangle with Calvin probably doesn't deserve to keep all their body parts."

My mother looked confused.

"Mom, he's a full-grown male chimpanzee," I explained. "If he wanted to, he could rip a man's arm right out of the socket and then beat him over the head with it."

Now instead of confused she looked shocked.

"But he wouldn't do that," Mr. McCurdy reassured her. "Most likely he'll just lie down in the back seat and have a nap."

Almost as if Calvin had understood what Mr. McCurdy had said, he stretched, yawned, and plopped down on the seat.

"Shouldn't we be going?" I suggested.

"Yes, we should," my mother agreed.

"Take it easy, Calvin," Nick called out, and a long, hairy arm appeared and waved goodbye. Then Calvin sat up, puckered his lips, and blew us a big kiss before lying back down.

We picked up our bags, and Mr. McCurdy slammed the trunk shut with a thud. He tried to take one of my mother's bags, but she insisted she had to carry them both. We hurried into the terminal, moving as fast as we could with our luggage. There were people around, but it wasn't particularly crowded. Certainly not like it would have been in a big airport. I wondered how busy it would be at the other end.

Saying goodbye to Mom was a lot harder than saying goodbye to Calvin. There were real kisses and even a few tears, mostly from

Mom and me. I could tell Nick was working hard not to let us see he was fighting back tears. He always had to be so cool.

We all stood at the big glass window and waved as Mom got onto the plane. When it inched away from the terminal, we kept waving. We didn't know if she was on the side of the plane where she could see us, but we had a fifty-fifty chance. I kept watching as it started down the runway, and then I began to say a silent prayer. Takeoffs and landings are the most dangerous times—I'd read that somewhere. The plane started to really move now, faster and faster, and then it separated from the ground and jumped into the air. I continued to watch, trying to keep it safe, until it became smaller and smaller and finally disappeared.

I turned around and saw Mr. McCurdy standing right there beside Nick. For a few seconds I'd forgotten he was even there, and I had a sudden rush of gratitude. I knew I didn't really need him there, but it was nice just the same.

"She'll miss you, too," Mr. McCurdy said. "Now let's get you two over to your gate for boarding before you miss your plane."

"Missing our flight would be okay," Nick said.

"No, it wouldn't," I said.

"We could stay at home or even with Mr. McCurdy."

"Nick," I cautioned.

"Maybe we wouldn't even have to tell Mom we didn't go and then—"

"Nick," Mr. McCurdy growled, cutting him off.

"Okay, okay, you can't blame a guy for trying, can you?"

"Don't go worrying none, Nick." Mr. McCurdy said. "Your girl-friend can do just fine without you for a week."

"You know he has a girlfriend?" I questioned.

"I've met her."

"You have? When, where?"

"Oh, about a month or so ago. Nick brought her out to my place."

"Where was I?" I asked.

"Band practice, or something silly like that," Nick said. "Tori's mother offered to drive me home from school, and on the way we stopped at Mr. McCurdy's to see the animals."

"That was nice of her mother to drive out of the way like that." Nick laughed. "She suggested it!"

"But how did she know about...?" I let the sentence trail off. There probably wasn't anybody in our whole area who didn't know about Mr. McCurdy and his animals. It had been such a big story in the newspapers, then an issue in the election for the mayor, and a big story again when he was finally given permission to keep his animals.

"She's a nice lady," Mr. McCurdy said. "She really liked Buddha."

"She even wanted to go into the cage with him," Nick added.

"She did?" I asked.

Mr. McCurdy shook his head. "Told her no. Until Buddha knows somebody well it isn't bright to let them into the cage."

"But you let me in the cage when I didn't know him very well," I said.

"That was different. I knew you and that tiger would get along fine. Now let's get to that plane before Nick gets what he wants and the two of you have to stay here."

We started off across the terminal. Our flight was leaving from a gate on the far side of the building. Of course, it wasn't a very big building, so it would only take a couple of minutes to cross the entire length.

I dug my hand into the pocket of my jacket and pulled out our tickets. I'd already looked at them ten or twelve times. Two tickets, each reading flight 1336, gate 12, boarding 10:35, departure 11:05.

We stopped directly in front of the security check by the gate. Mr. McCurdy couldn't go any farther than this. There were people milling around, sitting in the seats, standing, waiting to go through.

"Do you two have gum for the flight?" Mr. McCurdy asked.

"I don't," I said.

"Me, neither," Nick agreed.

"Here," Mr. McCurdy said, pulling some change out of his pocket. "Go and get you and your sister some gum while Sarah and I have us a little talk."

That made me suspicious. What did Mr. McCurdy want to talk to me about that he didn't want Nick to hear? Nick took the money and went off toward the store. I sat in the seat beside the one Mr. McCurdy had taken.

"Now, Sarah, I want you to know everything's going to be fine. There's nothing for you to be worried about."

"I'm not worried...much."

"Are you nervous about taking care of Nick?"

"A little."

"You know there'll be staff people there to be in charge. All you've got to do is get the two of you off the plane at the other end and you don't have to worry about him anymore."

"I know," I said, even though I knew that no matter how many staff there were at this camp I'd still feel as if I was in charge of him.

"And if anything were to happen, and we know it won't, they'd just get hold of your mother or your aunt—or me."

"You?"

"Do you think I'm too old to help sort things out if there's a problem?"

"Of course not, but it's pretty far away," I said.

"Where is this place?" Mr. McCurdy asked.

"I don't know exactly...hold on a second...Mom gave me a couple of brochures about the place," I said as I dug into my carry-on luggage. I pulled them out and handed one to Mr. McCurdy.

"You can hang on to that one if you want," I said.

"This isn't that far," he said as he put his finger on the address on the back of the brochure. "I could be there by car in less than a day."

"But even if I needed to, how could we get in touch with you? You don't have a phone."

"You got a point there." He paused. "You have your friend Erin's telephone number, don't you?"

"Yeah." I had all my friends' numbers in my head.

"Then if you have any problems you call Erin, and she'll come and tell me you need to talk to me."

"That would work."

"Course it would. And if you think about it, I might even be *the* best person for you to contact if there's a problem."

I gave him a questioning look.

"Think about it. Your aunt lives pretty well on the other side of the country and has her own family to take care of, right?"

"Three kids."

"And your mother, once they get a message through to her, is just as far away." He paused. "'Sides, don't you think she deserves a week without worry?"

I nodded. That was something I thought everybody needed but some of us never got.

"So if you have a problem, just call Erin and she'll tell me. I'll take care of everything. Okay?"

Again I nodded. "Thanks."

"No need to thank me. Helping each other out is what family's all about."

Family...I liked the sound of that.

"I don't know why everybody complains about airplane food," Nick said as he shovelled in the last of his meal. "This is really good!"

He had eaten his meal at the speed of light. I realized it wasn't that big a meal, but the speed that he'd devoured it with had amazed me. I was picking away at mine slowly.

"Don't you like yours?" he asked.

"You may be the only person in the whole world who likes airplane food."

"If you don't like it, can I have yours?"

"No, you can't!" I said indignantly.

"But if you don't like it, then why can't I have it?"

"Because it's mine, and it's all I have."

I dug my fork in and took another small piece. I thought that it was chicken, or maybe fish. I was certain it wasn't beef...or almost certain.

"Do you think they'll feed us at camp?" Nick asked.

"No, Nick, they're going to starve us for a whole week."

"I mean, are they going to feed us as soon as we get there?"

"How would I know?"

"I don't know. You just seem to know everything...or at least *think* you know everything."

"Thanks," I said sarcastically. "Here, have a look at this." I pulled the last copy of the camp brochure out of my bag. "It mentions something about meals."

Nick grabbed it from my hands. "Where'd you get that from?"

"A couple of copies came in the mail a few days ago. I gave Mr. McCurdy one."

He opened it and started to read. I'd already looked through it. It certainly wasn't very professional-looking. It looked like somebody had made it up on their home computer—their home computer without a spell checker. I'd counted four spelling mistakes, not to mention how badly it was organized, and it had no pictures and—

"This actually doesn't sound bad," Nick said. "They have more animals than Mr. McCurdy."

"It's a zoo camp, so wouldn't that be expected?"

"I guess...I mean, I just hadn't thought about it much."

"You never think of anything much."

"Seriously, it says they have all kinds of big cats...not just a tiger, but lions, jaguars, some leopards, a bear and—"

"What kind of bear?" I asked. I'd only browsed the brochure myself, and I didn't like bears.

"It doesn't say," Nick answered, not looking up from the brochure. "And they also have some of buffalo, a herd of deer, birds of prey, and—wow, this is unbelievable!"

"What?"

"They have three elephants!" Nick practically screamed.

People in the seats across the aisle turned and stared at us. I looked away. There probably wasn't anybody on the plane who hadn't heard him.

"I'm personally more interested in other things than the animals," I said through clenched teeth.

"What could be more interesting than elephants—except for maybe a whale?" Nick asked in amazement.

"Things like where we're going to being staying."

Nick shrugged. "That's not very interesting. Besides, it says right here that we're going to be staying in rustic accommodations. What's a rustic?"

I shook my head. "Rustic isn't a type of place. It *describes* the place. It means like not modern or fancy...old."

"Like a cabin?" Nick asked.

"Or a shack," I muttered.

Nick snickered, "And you said I was being silly about the food. They're not going to be putting us in a shack, Sarah."

I knew he was right. I hated it when he was right and wanted to change the subject. "I guess having elephants is pretty exciting."

"I can't wait until I'm sitting on top of one of them and—"

"You may have a long, long, wait," I cautioned.

"This is only a two-hour flight, and the camp can't be that far from the airport, so how long can it be?"

"Not long until we get there, but no telling how long before they let you ride on the elephant...if they ever do."

"Why wouldn't they?" Nick demanded.

"Because they can't just let some kids loose around an elephant."

"But we're not just some kids! We're experienced around exotic animals. We'll tell them about Mr. McCurdy and his animals and all the time we spend at his farm with Buddha, Laura, and Calvin."

"Just because we've spent time with some exotic animals doesn't mean they'll let us near these ones."

"So you mean we could come all this way and not be allowed as close to these animals as we are to Mr. McCurdy's?" Nick questioned in disbelief.

"That could happen. They may not even believe us when we say we've spent time around a tiger. If somebody told you they spent time every day with a tiger, wouldn't you think they were making the whole thing up?"

"Well, I don't know, maybe, maybe not."

"Think about it, Nick. It's not a normal sort of thing to have a tiger for your next-door neighbour."

"But we do. We'll just have to convince them—you'll have to convince them."

"Why me?"

"Because people believe you. You have such an honest face."

"Thank you."

"And that's good because you really aren't very good at lying."

"That's not true! I can—" I stopped myself. It seemed pretty stupid to be arguing that I was a good liar. Especially when I wasn't. Nick was a different matter. He was quick on his feet and could say practically anything with a straight face.

"So, will you talk to them, Sarah?"

"I'll talk to them, but even if they do believe me about Buddha and the other animals, that doesn't mean they'll let you anywhere near their elephants."

"Why not? I've never had any problems with elephants at Mr. McCurdy's place," Nick said.

"Mr. McCurdy doesn't have any elephants."

Nick smiled. "Well, you know that, and I know that, but nobody at this camp knows that."

"Didn't you just say I was bad at lying? Now you're asking me to lie for you?"

"I'm not asking you to lie."

"Good, because—"

"I can handle that all by myself. All I'm asking you to do is say nothing."

"And if they ask me?" I questioned.

"Just say you've never, ever, seen me have a single problem with an elephant."

"I told you I'm not lying for you!"

"And I told you I didn't want you to. Have you ever seen me with an elephant?" he asked.

"No."

"Then if you've never seen me with an elephant, how could you ever see me have a *problem* with one?"

"Nicholas Eric Fraser...sometimes you are such a little—"

"Could I please have your attention!" a flight attendant said over the PA. "We will be landing shortly. Can passengers please finish their meals so the trays and seats can be returned to the upright position. Thank you."

"Now if you'll stop bothering me, I have to finish my meal."

"You make it sound like all I ever do is bother you," Nick said defensively.

"Well?"

"Come on, Sarah, I can be helpful. I could help you right now."

"You could? How could you help me?"

"For starters, I can help you finish your meal."

❖

"How do we even know who we're looking for?" Nick asked as

we stood at the baggage carousel and waited for our luggage to appear.

It was a good question. I scanned the crowd, hoping an obvious answer would jump out at me. "Maybe they'll be holding up a sign that'll say ZOO CAMP."

"I don't see any sign like that," Nick said.

Neither did I. There had been one person who had been holding a sign over his head. That's where I'd gotten the idea. That sign had somebody's name written on it, and the two people had connected and then left.

What I did see were hundreds of people. Some were sitting, others walking and moving through the terminal, others waiting for people to arrive, and lots like us, standing at the luggage carousel, waiting for their bags to appear. Those of us by the carousel reminded me of a bunch of vultures perched on limbs, waiting for something to die.

"What if nobody comes to get us?" Nick asked.

"Somebody will. Don't worry," I said, sounding confident. How I sounded and how I felt were worlds apart. Either way, though, there was no need for Nick to worry. Worrying was my job. "Let's just do first things first and get our luggage."

Almost on cue I was startled by the sound of the luggage carousel rumbling to life. The large metal sections of the conveyor glided along, squeaking slightly as they rounded the corners. There was a loud *clunk* and the first bag slid down and landed on the conveyor. It was followed immediately by a second bag, and a third, and a fourth.

This was good. Once all the luggage had come people would grab their bags and leave. Eventually all that would be left would be us and whoever was here to pick us up. Quickly bags were grabbed from the carousel and thrown over shoulders or onto little grocery-cart type things, or simply carried away. Regardless, with each bag taken, another person walked away, thinning out the group.

"There's my bag!" Nick cried

"Go and get it."

Nick ran over, grabbed it, and threw it at his feet. "And there's yours!" he said, chasing it down and hauling it off the conveyor, as well.

Bag by bag, the crowd was quickly getting smaller. I started looking more intensely at the remaining people. I spied an older man with a beard, wearing a beat-up old hat that looked as if it had been chewed on by a tiger. He looked like an animal guy. Maybe I should just walk over and see if he was from the camp and—a woman ran to him and he gave her a big hug and a kiss. If he was one of the zoo camp staff, he was a lot more friendly than I wanted. The man and woman walked off, pushing a cart full of luggage.

Well, if it wasn't him, maybe it was...my second choice, another man wearing a safari-type jacket. But he started to walk away with his luggage. Person after person left. What had started as encouraging, getting rid of the extra people, was now getting scary. There was hardly anybody left, and worst of all, none of them seemed to be looking for us. The last few people grabbed their bags and left.

I watched as the luggage carousel went round and round and round—it was completely empty. There was no more baggage to be picked up, and no more people. With a loud thud the conveyor belt came to a stop. It was now official.

"What now, Sarah?" There was something about his tone of voice that was different than usual. He sounded anxious.

"Maybe we should look outside," I said. "They could be waiting for us out there."

That may not have been my brightest idea, but it was the only one I had. What would we do if we got outside and there was nobody? What then? We could always wait...but for how long? I guess we could find a security guard or maybe a police officer and tell him what happened. They'd help us, make a call—

a call to Erin to get Mr. McCurdy—and he could come and get us. But even if we got through to Erin, and she went straight to Mr. McCurdy, he couldn't possibly get here today. He was more than eight hundred kilometres away. Maybe we could use our return ticket today, and he could meet us at the airport. But if we couldn't, if there wasn't a flight today, then where would we stay until then? Who would be in charge of us?

I put a hand against my pocket. There were six twenty-dollar bills folded in there. That was my baby-sitting money, and I'd brought it along, just in case. I knew Nick probably didn't have two nickels in his pockets. He spent his money slightly faster than he got it. If worse came to worse, we could always stay the night in a hotel. I was old enough to take care of Nick for one night.

"Come on, Nick, let's go outside to check."

I picked up my bags and started to walk. I'd gone no more than a half-dozen steps when I stopped dead in my tracks. There, hidden from where we were standing by the luggage carousel, were two kids—a boy and a girl. The girl was about Nick's age, and the boy was a few years younger. I'd noticed them a couple of times while we were waiting, but hadn't paid much attention to them. It wasn't as if they were there to meet us. Obviously, whoever was picking them up was late, too. They were just standing there beside their luggage by themselves. They looked worried. I was sure they'd be picked up soon and...what if...

"Excuse me!" I called out, and they both looked over. "Are you two going to zoo camp?"

In answer they both came toward us. The little boy looked scared. The girl had her hands on her hips and looked angry.

"You should have been here right away to meet us," the girl said, wagging a finger at me. "You scared my brother! We thought we'd got off the plane at the wrong place, or should have been waiting someplace else."

"We were worried," the boy said, wiping a tear away with

the back of his hand.

"I'm sorry you were scared, but—"

"But you should have been here on time!" the girl snapped. "I was going to call out to the camp," she said, holding up a cell phone I hadn't noticed in her hand. "But I couldn't find a phone number on the brochure. Why didn't you put one on?"

"That's strange, not having a telephone number," Nick said.

"So, are we going straight to the camp or waiting for other people?" she asked.

I didn't even know this kid's name, but I'd already taken a definite dislike to her.

"Oh, we're going to be waiting," Nick said. "Waiting for somebody to pick us up."

"I don't understand," the girl said. "Aren't you going to drive us?"

"First, I'm not old enough to drive," I told her. "And second, I don't work at the camp."

"You don't?" The girl looked confused and worried. She took a couple of steps away from me. "But...but...how did you know we were going to zoo camp?"

"When we saw that nobody had picked you up, and nobody had picked us up, then I just thought that—"

"Because we're going to zoo camp, too," Nick said.

"You're a kid?" the girl asked, pointing at me.

"I'm not a kid...I'm almost fifteen. But I'm going to camp. My name is Sarah, and this is my brother, Nicholas."

"Nick," he said.

"I'm Samantha, and this is my little brother, Daniel."

"Danny," he said. "I'm Danny."

"I guess we're all in the same boat," I said.

"Boat?" Danny asked, looking around.

"It's a figure of speech," his sister said. "It just means we're all in the same situation."

"We were going to go outside and see if somebody was waiting for us out there," I explained. "Do you want to come with us?"

"I think we should wait right here. That would be the *smart* thing to do," she said, implying that I was doing the stupid thing.

"Suit yourself. You can spend the entire week right here, for all I care."

"I want to go with her," Danny whined.

She let out a big sigh. "Fine, we'll go with them. Just wait while we get all our luggage."

They went back to get their bags. She had two huge pieces of luggage and partially carried, partially dragged, them toward us.

"How long are you going to be at this camp?" I asked.

"A week," she said. "I try to be prepared."

Again, there was something about her tone of voice or the expression on her face that said she was right and anybody else who didn't have two bags was wrong.

"Do you want a hand?" Nick asked.

I turned to him in shock. Nick offering to help?

"You can take the big bag. The one that's slightly smaller has all my valuables in it."

"Valuables?" I asked. She was such a princess that I expected there must be a diamond-studded tiara in there somewhere with her underwear.

"My new digital camera, a CD player and, of course, my video camera," she said.

"That's cool," Nick said. "Do you think that I—"

"Do you think we can get going?" I asked, cutting him off.

Nobody said another word, and we started for the big set of doors. Just outside there was a line of taxis. Beyond that was a busy street and cars sitting at parking meters and—there it was! A large van with the words ZOO CAMP painted on its side!

Chapter 3

"There it is!" I screamed.

"What? Where's what?" Nick demanded.

"The van from the camp," I said, pointing toward it.

They all saw it at once, and there was a rush toward the road.

"Hold on!" I said, grabbing Danny's arm. "This is a busy street and we have to be careful and cross at the lights."

"You sound like my big sister," he said.

"All big sisters sound alike," Nick said.

"Maybe we all sound the same because all little brothers are the same," Samantha said.

"What do you mean by that?" Nick asked.

"Irresponsible little goofs who have to be taken care of!"

"Hey, I resent that!" Nick protested.

"I think you resemble that comment more than you resent it," I said.

We went over to the crossing and waited for the light to change. I kept one eye on the signal and the other on the van. The last thing I wanted was for it to take off when we weren't looking. It remained at the curb while the light changed and we crossed. It wasn't going anywhere.

As we got closer, I got a better look at the van. It was pretty beat-up with dents, bangs, and rust spots. A big crack in the windshield radiated like a spiderweb. The logo on the side of the vehicle—ZOO CAMP—looked as if it was painted by the same person who had created the brochure. Different letters were different sizes, and the edges weren't clear or clean.

"Nobody's here," Nick said.

"Maybe they're inside the airport looking for us," Samantha said. She still believed we should have waited inside and didn't want to admit I was right in suggesting we come out.

"Maybe they are inside," I agreed. "But if we wait right here, they're bound to come back. We'll just wait here and—*ahhh!*" I screamed as I recoiled from the van.

A man had suddenly appeared in the driver's seat! I stumbled back a few more feet. The man's head and face were a tangled mat of hair, beard, and moustache. He opened the door and climbed out of the truck. He was gigantic, and I took a few more steps away, almost tripping over my luggage. The man was dressed in dirty old jeans and a T-shirt and had black rubber boots on his feet.

"You kids look for zoo camp?" he asked in a heavy accent.

Everybody nodded.

"Climb in van."

We all hesitated. How did we even know he was the staff person?

"Hurry, hurry," he said, gesturing with his hands. "You want help with lug...with lug...with bags?"

Nobody moved. He paused, and his face twisted into a thoughtful look. "Don't be 'fraid...nothing to fear. Me Vladimir," he said, pointing to his chest. "From camp. I waiting for you to come. You are—" He pulled a piece of paper out of his pocket and unfolded it. "You Danny, Samantha, Sarah, and Nicolai."

"Nick," my brother said. "It's Nick."

"In English it is Nick. In Russia it is Nicolai, like Czar Nicolai."

"What's a czar?" Nick asked.

"It means like a president or a prime minister," I said.

"More like a king," Samantha said, correcting me. "They

were the royal family of Russia."

"I like that," Nick said. "Royalty. King Nicolai."

"You're more like the court jester," I said.

"Come, I take bags," Vladimir said.

With one hand he grabbed Danny's bag and tucked it under his arm, then took one of Samantha's bags and Nick's. The way he picked them up you would have thought they were empty. He tossed them into the back of the van, turned around, grabbed my suitcase, and did the same.

"I fix bags...you get in van."

Nick pulled open the sliding door and climbed in, with Danny following. I was just about to open the passenger door when Samantha grabbed it and climbed into the seat. I was going to sit there! She should be sitting in the back—she was younger than me. I looked back at Vladimir securing the luggage. Maybe it would be better not to sit right beside him. I climbed in and took the middle seat.

The inside of the van wasn't much better than the outside. The seats were old, ripped, and made of some sort of fake blue leather that felt sticky in the heat. I shouldn't complain. At least we were in the right place, or at least in the right place to get to the right place. Well, at least I was pretty sure this was the right place. He must work for the zoo camp—although what if he didn't? What if he was some deranged mental patient who had killed the staff person, or stolen the van, or just painted his van to look like this? That would explain the paint job. But how would he know our names if he wasn't from the camp?

Vladimir climbed into the driver's seat and plopped down. He turned the key, and the engine coughed and sputtered and tried hard to start—but didn't. Vladimir mumbled something in a language I didn't understand. Maybe it was Russian. He tried the engine again and it made a grinding sound. He said something else. This time, even though I still didn't understand the words, I figured I knew what he was saying.

Suddenly the engine came to life with a roar, and Vladimir

laughed and slammed his fist against the dashboard. Samantha and I both jumped. "Not good truck," he said. "Old...old like grandmother...but worse...grandmother strong like bear...truck not."

He turned the wheel and steered the truck into traffic. It chugged and rocked as he changed gears.

"Is the camp far from here?" I asked.

"Not far," he said. "Fifteen, twenty minutes' drive. There soon."

"We would be there already if you'd come in to get us," Samantha said. She certainly had a lot of nerve.

"Have to wait by truck. Parking here at air place is much money. No money if I stay by truck. I figure you come out soon or later."

"But we didn't see you when we first came out," I said.

"Lying down in seat...sleep...very tired...up night last."

"You didn't sleep last night?" Samantha asked.

He shook his head. "Working all night."

"You were working all night?" I questioned. "Couldn't whatever it is have waited until today?"

"I ask lion. She say no. She wanted to have babies in night."

"One of your lions had a cub!" I almost yelled.

"Not cub...four babies."

"Wow! That's wonderful!"

"Season for babies."

"And you actually got to watch a lion give birth?" Nick said, sounding amazed.

"Not watch...help."

"You helped her?" I asked. Now it was my turn to be amazed.

He nodded.

"Are you a veterinarian?" Samantha asked.

Vladimir burst into laughter, and the whole van seemed to shake. "I no doctor of animals."

"But wouldn't it have been better to have a qualified veterinarian there in case something went wrong?" Samantha pressed.

"Vets are for pets...for poodles. For *real* animals you need real animal man."

"Like Mr. McCurdy!" Nick exclaimed.

Vladimir's look was questioning.

"He's a friend of ours," I explained.

"And friend is animal man?" Vladimir asked.

"Are you kidding?" Nick said. "He has a tiger, a chimpanzee, a big Burmese python, and a cheetah."

"Cheetah? He has cheetah?" Vladimir asked.

"Yeah," I confirmed. "Her name's Laura."

"Cheetahs not common. Where he get cheetah?"

"He raised her, and her mother, and lots of other cheetahs—"

"He raised cheetahs?" Vladimir interrupted, practically turning around in his seat to look at me. "Nobody have cheetah babies."

"Practically nobody. Mr. McCurdy did, though," I said, pointing at the windshield. "The road!"

"See road. And man have zoo?"

"It's not a zoo. Mr. McCurdy and his animals live on the farm right beside our farm."

"And he raise cheetahs on farm?"

"Not on the farm. He did that when he was with the carnival," I said.

"Carnival is like circus!" Vladimir bellowed. "Like Vladimir! Vladimir worked in circus in Russia!"

"Mr. McCurdy always said how exciting it was to do that sort of work. I bet it would be even more exciting to work in a Russian circus," I said.

"Friend...Mr. Mc...Mc..."

"Mr. McCurdy," I said.

"*Da, da,* Mr. McCurdy. I would like to meet man who raised cheetahs. Can I meet?"

"Sure, he likes visitors, and I bet he'd like to meet another circus man," I said.

"How far away he live?"

"Not far. About a two-hour flight."

"Vladimir not like planes. Planes small, have to duck head to get in, and Vladimir not fit in seats." That probably had more to do with the size of Vladimir than it did the size of the planes.

"You could drive there," Nick suggested. "I bet you could drive it in a day."

"No car."

"Couldn't you use this van?" Nick asked.

"Not good for driving."

Nobody would argue with that. The engine, which had been thumping badly the whole time, sounded as if it were going to shoot right through the hood whenever we started to climb a hill. Behind us we trailed a cloud of blue smoke. To top it off, it seemed to me that the whole van was tilting toward Vladimir. Maybe that was partially because he was so big, but still, it shouldn't have been leaning in his direction.

"Maybe you could take a bus," Nick suggested.

"Much money. 'Sides, no time. Have to work."

"You could go when you have a vacation," Nick said.

"What is vacation?" Vladimir asked.

"Holidays...time off," Nick answered.

Vladimir snorted. "No time off with animals. Animals need Vladimir."

"Couldn't one of the other staff take care of the animals while you were gone?" Nick was one persistent guy. Actually, he persistently annoyed me with his persistence.

"No other people."

"You're the only staff person at this camp?" I questioned anxiously.

"Other people. No other animal people. People sell tickets, clean garbage."

"Well, you'll have lots of help this week," Nick said. "Because of Mr. McCurdy, Sarah and I know lots about animals."

"Which girl Sarah?" Vladimir asked.

"Me, I'm Sarah."

"And I'm Samantha."

Vladimir nodded. "Little girl Samantha...big girl Sarah."

"I'll help, too. My name's Danny," the little boy chimed in.

"I'm sure all the campers will help," Samantha said. "How many are there?"

"Four," Vladimir said.

"Four?" I questioned.

"Da."

"But there has to be more than four," I argued.

"Maybe I have wrong word for right number," Vladimir said. "One...two...three, and four. Four in truck."

"We know there are four people in the van, but how many are in the camp?" I asked.

"Four. One, two, three, four," he said, pointing at us as he counted. "You all campers."

"But there has to be more campers," Samantha argued.

"Maybe next week. First week four. One, two, three—"

"We get the idea," Samantha snapped.

She certainly was sharp with people, more than a little bossy, and a bit of a know-it-all. But I couldn't waste my time thinking about her when I had bigger concerns. What sort of a camp had a beat-up old van, basically one staff member, and only four campers? It must be something else.

"Can we see the baby lions when we get there?" Nick asked from the back of the van.

"Can see, but not close," Vladimir said. "People close make lion mummy 'fraid, and if 'fraid she could kill babies."

"Kill them?" Samantha cried.

Vladimir shrugged. "Happen sometimes. We leave babies and mummy alone for while."

"That's too bad," Nick said. "It would be neat to see them when they're that young."

"Lots of babies still come. This is time...how you say...season. You may even help with some mummies and babies."

That sounded sort of exciting. And scary. And probably messy.

"Here is camp!" Vladimir called out, and the bus slowed down.

Chapter 4

We were passing by a long, high, white wooden wall. On the wall were gigantic paintings of animals. Some were sitting, others standing, jumping, sitting in trees, or partially hidden in jungle scenes. They were certainly colourful, but not much better than the paintings on the side of the van.

Vladimir turned the van into a lane and stopped in front of a high chain-link gate. It was topped by strands of barbed wire. He climbed out of the van, and the whole thing seemed to rise, relieved of his weight. Vladimir walked up to the gate, removed a thick chain, and gave the gate a good push. It swung open, inviting us to enter.

Vladimir came back to the van, got in, and put it into gear. It rumbled a few feet forward, sputtered, and stalled halfway through the gate. He tried to restart the van, but the engine coughed and complained. As he turned the key again, the engine cranked but wouldn't catch. Vladimir muttered under his breath. The engine wasn't listening to what he was saying—whatever it was—and continued to grind.

"Everybody out!" Vladimir ordered.

I guessed we were at the end of the line, and was grateful the old bucket of bolts had gotten us this far. We started to climb out.

"Wait!" Vladimir called out, and everybody froze. "Big

girl...Sarah...you not get out. You steer."

"Steer? What do you mean steer?"

"You steer while rest push."

"We're going to push the van?" Nick asked.

"Cannot leave here. Must push."

"But I don't know how to drive," I protested.

"Not drive. Steer."

Vladimir climbed out and patted the seat with his hand, motioning me to sit. Reluctantly I moved between the seats and plunked down.

"Good, now steer."

I put both hands on the steering wheel. Vladimir closed the door and joined everybody else at the back of the van.

"Ready!" Vladimir yelled. "Now push!"

I braced myself, getting ready for the vehicle to move. Vladimir, I figured, was probably strong enough by himself to hurl the van forward. I tightened my grip on the wheel and...it didn't move.

Vladimir walked to the side of the van and tapped on the window. I rolled down the glass, and he leaned in.

"Sarah need to take foot off brake."

"Oh, I'm sorry," I apologized as I moved my foot.

The vehicle started to roll backward.

"Put foot back on brake!" he bellowed.

I jumped and slammed my foot down at the same time, wishing he hadn't yelled.

"Keep foot on brake till I tell to push," he said, returning to the back of the van. "Push!"

I lifted my foot, and the van started moving—not quickly, but it definitely was inching forward. I held on to the wheel even tighter. The van picked up speed and we cleared the gate. The whole park opened before me. There were pens and some buildings down the road—far enough away that there was no chance I could hit them.

The van continued to pick up speed. Boy, were they ever pushing hard! I wondered how far they wanted to go. Maybe to that first building. Every foot closer meant a foot less we had to carry our luggage.

I looked in the rearview mirror. They weren't pushing—they were far behind, running and waving their arms! My stomach did a flip! I realized I was going down a slight hill that led all the way to the buildings—and I was rolling, picking up speed, going faster and faster! I slammed my foot on the brake. The van screeched to a stop and, to my shock, I continued forward, soaring out of my seat over the steering wheel and toward the windshield. Helpless, I tried to free my hands from the wheel, but I could only slightly turn my head as the side of my face smacked into the glass. I bounced back and landed in the seat again.

That hurt like crazy, but at least I'd managed to...the van started forward again slowly. I jammed my foot back onto the brake. There had to be some way to keep it from rolling without my keeping my foot there. I thought about my mother driving and all the times I'd watched her and...the emergency brake! I looked to the side, saw the little pedal, pushed it down, and locked it into place. When I removed my foot, the van stayed still.

Opening the door, I climbed out. The others were still down the road and were now walking. I bent down and looked at my face in the side-view mirror. I couldn't see anything—no cut, or bruising—at least not yet, but it still felt sore as I rubbed the side of my face. The only good thing was that Nick hadn't been there to laugh about it.

"We thought you were stealing the van!" Nick yelled as they closed in.

"I just figured I'd save us from having to carry the bags so far."

Vladimir opened the back door and started to pull out our luggage. I circled around the side and joined everybody else.

"Do we have to carry our things much farther?" Samantha asked.

"Not far," Vladimir said, pointing toward a large house.

I'd stopped the van almost directly in front of it. The house looked really fancy. Maybe this wouldn't be so bad. We grabbed our bags. All I wanted to do was unpack and take a bath. It wasn't just that I wanted to get clean. I also needed a door that would lock with me on one side and Nick and the rest of the world on the other. Maybe because there were only four of us I'd even have my own bathroom.

"This is some place," Nick said. "It certainly doesn't look like a shack."

That last comment was aimed at me. This was one of the few times in my life that I was glad Nick was right and I was wrong.

"Big, new house," Vladimir said.

"Was it built especially for the campers?" Samantha asked.

"Campers?" Vladimir asked.

"For us," I said. "The kids who are coming to stay here."

"Not for you. For owners."

"So we're not staying there?" I questioned, stating the obvious.

"*Nyet*...um, no. You stay—come, follow."

We trudged behind him. My bags seemed to be gaining weight with each step. My only consolation was that while it was hard for me, it was twice as hard for Samantha with her two big suitcases. Hopefully we didn't have to go much farther. Vladimir led us through the clearing and onto another path leading off to the side. At the end I could see another building. It wasn't fancy or new. It looked sort of like a cottage, which was what I'd expected, anyway. It wasn't big, but it was kind of cute.

"So this is it," I said.

"*Nyet*. This is where Vladimir sleep. You sleep there," he said, pointing toward the end of the clearing. There were three buildings. As we got closer, I could see that they weren't just little, but run-down. One even had a broken window, a piece of cardboard replacing the pane of glass.

"Come look," Vladimir said as he stepped up onto the little

wooden porch of the middle of the three buildings. It seemed to sag under his weight. Vladimir opened the front door, and it squeaked loudly. He entered, with Nick, Samantha, and Daniel following. I wasn't sure if this little building could hold five of us and all our luggage, but there was no way I was waiting outside.

The inside was tiny but neat. There were two sets of bunk beds on opposite walls. Between them were two dressers, a little table, and three chairs tucked underneath.

"You stay here," Vladimir said.

"All of us?" Samantha asked.

"*Da*. Four kids, four beds."

"But what about the other two cabins? Couldn't somebody else sleep in one of those?" I questioned.

"Not ready yet."

"You mean they need the beds made, or to be dusted, or something? I could do that," I volunteered.

"Need more than bed made. Need windows replaced or roof fixture to not leak when rains. Vladimir will fix before more kids come, but not now."

"It's not a big deal," Danny said. "We're not going to be spending much time in here, anyway."

"He's right," Nick agreed. "Besides, all that's really important is that I get the top bunk!" Nick put a dirty foot on the lower bunk and heaved himself onto the top bed.

"I got the other!" Danny screamed. He threw his bag onto the top of the second set of beds, then quickly climbed up to join it.

"I don't care which bed I'm in," I said as I plopped onto the bed beneath Nick.

"Neither do I," Samantha agreed.

That was good, because there was only one bed left.

"I have to go to the washroom," Samantha said. "Where is it?"

Vladimir pointed out the door. "Go to side and around back. You find in forest."

"The bathroom is outside?" Samantha gasped.

"Not outside. In building. Little building."

"It's an outhouse?" Nick asked in disbelief.

"Not out of house. In little building. Not bad. Vladimir use for years."

"Your place doesn't have a toilet, either?"

"Toilet in place where Vladimir live now. Vladimir live here for over three years. When boss build new house, I get old house of boss."

"That was nice of your boss," I said.

He shrugged. "New place because new boss come."

"But that was still very nice of him," I suggested.

Vladimir snorted. "Old boss was nice. New boss is son of old boss."

"What happened to the father?" I asked, although I was pretty sure what the answer was going to be. "Did he retire?"

"Not retire. Dead."

"I...I'm sorry."

"Vladimir sorry, too. Old boss was nice man...good man. Man who know much about animals. He love animals like family."

"I guess it was lucky his family, his son, felt the same way," I said.

Vladimir looked confused. "I don't understand."

"Well, I just figured that since he took over the park, he must like animals a lot, too."

Vladimir didn't answer. He had a look on his face that was...different.

"How long since the father died?" Samantha asked, ending the silence.

"Died during summer...almost twelve months ago."

"And did you know him for long?"

"He sponsored me to come from Russia. For three years we work together. Always together."

"You must have gotten to know him pretty well," I said.

"Know well. Know lots." He paused. "Enough talk. Vladimir

has work to do. Unpack and then you come."

Nick jumped down from the bunk bed. He pulled open the top drawer of the dresser and, in one motion, grabbed his bag, unsnapped it, turned it upside down, and dumped the contents into the drawer. "I'm unpacked, so I can come now."

"I can unpack later," Danny added.

"So can I!" Samantha piped in.

Vladimir chuckled. "And you, big girl Sarah?"

Part of me really liked the idea of them all going away and letting me have at least a few minutes on my own, but what the heck. "I can unpack later, too."

⁂

"Can we see the elephants first?" Nick asked as we walked along with Vladimir.

"Can't see elephants."

"Why not?" Nick persisted.

"No elephants no more...just elephant...one elephant."

"But it said in that brochure that you had *three* elephants."

"Had three. Now one."

"But those brochures were just made up, weren't they?" I asked.

"*Da, da,* few weeks ago. Two elephants gone only few days."

"Where did they go to?" I asked. "They didn't...they didn't..."

"No, not die," Vladimir said. "Both young elephants, healthy elephants."

"Then what happened to them?" Nick asked.

"Sold."

"Somebody bought two elephants?" Samantha questioned. "I just can't imagine somebody buying a couple of elephants."

"Not some*body*. Some*thing*. Zoo. Other zoo."

"But why would *your* zoo get rid of them?" Nick asked.

"Maybe there wasn't enough space," Danny said.

"Lots of space."

"But why did you get rid of them then?" Nick asked again.

"Money."

"You couldn't afford to keep them?"

"Not money to keep. Money to go. Big animals go, get big money back. Enough talk. You want to see animals or not?"

"Of course!" I exclaimed.

"Good. Then look at Boo Boo."

"Boo Boo?"

Vladimir stopped and pointed into a cage. "Boo Boo the bear."

"I don't see any—*woooo!*" Nick screamed as a black blur shot up a tree in the middle of the pen, stopping at the very top of the trunk. It had to be thirty feet up.

"I've never even seen a squirrel that could climb that fast," I said.

"Boo Boo climb good." Vladimir smiled and rested his hands against the screening, looking up at the animal perched in the tree.

"He's big," Nick said. "Really big."

"Not so big," Vladimir said with a shrug. "Big bears are Russian brown bears. Much big."

"He looks pretty big to me," I said, agreeing with Nick.

Vladimir shook his head. "No big. Maybe six hundred pounds."

"I had no idea bears could climb that fast," I said, still amazed at the speed with which it had scaled the tree.

"Black bears climb good. Other bears...not so good. Old joke. You know difference between black bear and grizzly bear?"

"Um, the size and colour maybe."

"Yes, but other way. You run from bear and climb tree. If bear climbs up after you, then it is black bear." Vladimir paused, and a smile crept onto his face again. "If bear grab tree and shake till you fall down, then it grizzly."

I shuddered at the thought while Nick and Danny laughed along with Vladimir.

"How much bigger than Boo Boo is a grizzly?" Nick asked.

"Grizzly twice as big."

"I can't imagine any bear being twice as big as that," I said, gesturing at the tree.

"He doesn't look *that* big," Samantha said.

"He'd look a whole lot bigger if he was standing right in front of you," I said. She wasn't the only one who could be disagreeable.

"Would you like to see Boo Boo closer?" Vladimir asked.

"Yeah, that would be great!" Nick exclaimed, and the other two agreed.

I remained silent. The only way I could see that happening was if we went into the cage, and I didn't want to go into any cage with any bear—even if he was just a "small" bear.

"I get Boo Boo down tree," Vladimir said. He reached into his pocket and pulled something out. It was small, silvery, and shiny. He held it over his head. "Boo Boo! Look what I got!" he yelled, waving one hand above his head while pointing to the object with the other. "Boo Boo!"

At first the bear didn't seem to pay any attention. He appeared quite content at the top of the tree, staring into the distance. It was probably a good view.

Then the bear glanced down at us and cocked his head to one side, looking almost thoughtful. He started to edge down the tree, slowly, hesitantly. Then he began to pick up speed, coming down faster and faster until, a half-dozen feet from the bottom, he dropped and hit the ground running. My heart stopped, and my mouth fell open as this mass of black came racing toward us. I stepped back and gasped as he crashed into the bars. Boo Boo stood right up against the bars on his hind legs, his head high above me, his muzzle poking through. He opened his mouth to reveal incredibly large yellow teeth. I felt a rush of hot, foul breath, and he grunted. It wasn't the noise I'd expected from a bear. It sounded more like what a pig would make.

Then I noticed the front claws hooked through the bars.

They were curved, black, and unbelievably long. No wonder he could climb so well. Those claws would easily dig into a tree— or a person. A shudder ran the length of my body.

"Do you want this, Boo Boo?" Vladimir asked. He opened his hand, and I saw what he was holding. It was a chocolate Easter egg wrapped in silver foil!

Boo Boo snorted loudly, pressing his face harder against the bars so that his muzzle stuck out. His tongue snaked out even farther.

"Bear has sweet tooth," Vladimir said as he unwrapped the egg to reveal the chocolate inside.

"You feed the bear chocolate?" Samantha questioned. "That can't be very healthy."

"No worse than for you to eat chocolate. Little piece not hurt big bear."

"What does he normally eat?" I asked.

"Carrots, apples, potatoes, berries...little piece of meat. Also things tossed over fence by people. Boo Boo like popcorn and hamburgers."

He turned back to the bear and held the chocolate closer, but still well out of reach of the flicking tongue. The bear pushed harder, and the fencing bulged slightly outward as it strained to hold in his bulk and muscle.

"Boo Boo no get treat till Vladimir get kiss."

"A kiss from who?" Nick asked.

"From bear. Boo Boo is a girl bear. Pretty girl bear."

Vladimir stepped forward and leaned toward the bear. She pressed against the bars and her tongue darted out and started to lick his face.

"That's disgusting!" Samantha shrieked as Boo Boo gave Vladimir a complete face wash. For once I agreed with her.

Vladimir stepped back. "Boo Boo have bad, bad bear breath. Needs breath mint more than chocolate. He extended his hand, and the bear's tongue shot out and took the treat.

"Why is she losing so much fur?" Danny asked, pointing to a few clumps of thick, coarse black fur that clung to the fence and lay on the ground at the bear's feet.

"Grow in winter, lose in summer."

Danny nodded. "That's good. I was thinking it was something else, like she was sick maybe."

"Boo Boo healthy bear...healthy *old* bear."

"How old is she?" I asked.

"Nearly thirty years old."

"I didn't think bears lived that long." Actually, I had no idea how long bears lived.

"In wild not live long like that. In cages live long, and Boo Boo always live here."

"Her whole life?" Nick asked.

"Since little puppy."

"Puppy? Don't you mean cub?" I said.

Vladimir shrugged. "Forget English words sometimes."

I felt bad for correcting him. "Was she born right here?"

"Born in woods. Found by road when little. This little," Vladimir said, holding his hands out to form a small cup.

"That small! She couldn't have been very old."

"Five days, maybe week. I see pictures."

"Where was her mother?" I asked.

"Mother dead. Little Boo Boo found by man driving. Mother bear by side of road, dead...hit by truck."

"And she was brought here?"

"Brought here to be cared for by old boss. Everybody know he good with animals. He raise. Feed milk with eyedropper, then bottle."

"That's amazing," I said.

" 'Mazing—what word mean?"

"It means good, really good," I said.

"Sort of unbelievable, like something that wasn't supposed to happen," Nick added.

"Like word. 'Mazing that Boo Boo live. Old boss good with animals. He 'mazing."

I had the urge to correct him and explain that the word was *amazing*, but I kind of liked it that way.

"Old boss, he know animals. He care for them good. 'Mazing man." He paused. "More than animals. He know people. He treat them good, too."

Vladimir stopped talking and gazed off into the distance. I had the feeling he was thinking about that old boss, who was obviously much more than a boss. It was hard to lose people you cared for. It was funny. I had no idea what the "old boss" looked like, but I couldn't help picturing Mr. McCurdy.

"I think that because of Boo Boo we here."

"What do you mean?" I asked.

"Boo Boo was first animal here. All else follow. No Boo Boo, no zoo. No zoo, no me here, no you here. All because of Boo Boo."

"That makes her a special bear."

"Most special bear. Old boss would put Boo Boo on leash and take for walks down street."

"Do you do that?" I asked.

"Boo Boo only walk for old boss. She think old boss her mummy. Me, I not look like anybody's mummy," he said, laughing.

"Boo Boo must miss the walks," Nick said.

"And the man who used to walk her," I added.

"Boo Boo miss," Vladimir said, "All animals miss him."

"Speaking of the other animals, can we see some of them?" Nick asked. "Maybe the elephant?"

"Can see elephant, but not next. See tiger next. Big cat."

"I've walked a tiger before, lots of times," Nick said. It was the truth, but it still sounded as if he was bragging—or lying.

We waved goodbye to Boo Boo and followed Vladimir down the road.

"What's in that cage?" Danny asked as we passed by another pen.

"Trees."

"I meant what sort of animal," Danny said.

"No animal," Vladimir said. "Just tree. Dangerous, wild tree. Keep in cage so not escape."

"But, but..."

Vladimir laughed. Even though I still thought Vladimir was scary-looking, I was quickly learning that he loved to laugh.

"No animal now. Gone."

"It escaped?" I asked anxiously.

"No escape. Die. Old animal."

"What sort of animal was it?" Nick asked.

"Jaguar."

"Too bad. I've never been around a jaguar," Nick said.

"Not too bad. Good. You no want to be around this cat. Not nice cat. Spit, claw, not nice animal."

"Are all jaguars like that?" I asked.

"Not all. Some tame. This cat come from other zoo as big cat. Other people treat bad when little, so cat act bad when big. Other jaguars here nicer."

We continued to move, and I saw that while there were lots of pens, many of them were empty. At least they looked empty. If something was in there, it was certainly hiding well.

"Want to see tiger."

"Of course we do," I answered.

"This is pen," Vladimir said.

It was a large cage filled with trees and bushes. I scanned the pen, but I didn't see any tiger. This certainly was a big, beautiful area for it, though. That was good for the cat, but not good for somebody trying to see the animal. There were lots of places for him to hide.

"I don't see anything," Samantha said.

"Me, neither," Danny added.

"Are you sure he didn't get out?" Nick asked.

"Of course he hasn't!" I blurted. There was no way I could

know that, but I had a terrible rush of memory when he asked the question. Recapturing Mr. McCurdy's Buddha last summer was the only time I ever wanted to have to deal with an escaped tiger.

Vladimir leaned against the fence and craned his head, looking for the tiger.

"He's there...right?" I asked.

Vladimir didn't answer, and my heart did a flip.

"Kushna!" he yelled. "Kitty, kitty, kitty!"

If that wasn't the stupidest way to call a tiger, I didn't know what...and then the tiger appeared, standing up in some low bushes in the very centre of the pen.

Even from this distance he was obviously very large. Slowly he started to come toward us, picking his way around trees, bushes, and stumps. As he closed in, I was captured by his eyes. Gigantic yellow eyes shining out from his enormous face. He stopped and stretched, his belly practically brushing against the ground. He started to move again, slowly, deliberately, coming straight toward us. Despite having a fence between me and the tiger, I still felt a rush of apprehension. It was just like the feeling I had the first time I spied Buddha in Mr. McCurdy's barn.

Kushna pushed his head against the fencing. It was a massive face on a massive head. Vladimir reached his hand in and scratched the tiger behind the ears. That was where Buddha liked to be rubbed, too.

Standing right before my eyes, he seemed not just big but enormous. Was he bigger than Buddha? I couldn't really tell, but either way, I was planning to stay on the opposite side of the bars.

"Can I walk him?" Nick asked.

"You can not!" I answered

"I wasn't asking you, Sarah. Can I walk him, Vladimir?"

"And I already answered," I said. "You can't! It could be very dangerous!"

"Kushna is good tiger," Vladimir said, and Nick smiled smugly. "Most of the time," the Russian continued, and Nick's smile melted away.

"What do you mean, 'most of the time'?" I asked.

Vladimir shrugged. "Kushna has good days and bad days."

"He has bad days?"

"*Da*. Everybody have bad days, no?"

"Yeah, I guess."

"Can you tell when Kushna's having a bad day?" Nick asked.

"*Da, da*," Vladimir said, nodding enthusiastically. "He take swing at your head."

"At my head?"

"Big swing with big paw," Vladimir said.

"Can you tell if it's a bad day *before* he takes a swing at somebody's head?" Nick persisted.

Vladimir didn't answer right away. "Not usually," he said thoughtfully.

"Then there's no way you're going into that pen," I said to my brother, and surprisingly he didn't argue.

"Big girl Sarah right. Most animals good. Kushna good, but dangerous sometimes. We keep Kushna on other side bars today."

Kushna continued to rub against Vladimir's hand, and he started to talk to him in Russian—or at least what I thought was Russian. Then he put his face right by the cage, and the tiger began to lick him.

"He really likes you," I said.

"Kushna like Vladimir. Could go in cage and sleep and Kushna just cuddle."

"But you said he was dangerous," Nick said.

"Is...very ferocious."

"He certainly doesn't look ferocious."

"Sometimes animal act gentle, but very dangerous. Must never turn back or—"

"Vladimir!" a high-pitched voice called out.

We all turned in the direction of the voice. It was a woman— a young woman—and she was waving an arm over her head as she came toward us.

"Vladimir!" she called out again.

He meekly waved back, then turned to me. "Some animals much more dangerous than others."

Chapter 5

"I've been looking for you everywhere!" the strange woman called out as she tottered unsteadily toward us on high heels. She was clad in a tight leopard-skin outfit. Even her shoes matched, as did the bow in her hair, which was blond, teased, and piled high on her head. Even from this distance I could tell she was wearing a lot of makeup.

The woman stumbled, then regained her balance. I guess high heels and gravel weren't the best combination in the world. Vladimir muttered something under his breath, and Samantha, Danny, and I all turned around. Whatever he'd said, he didn't repeat it.

"Who is she?" I asked Vladimir quietly.

"Owner."

"But I thought the new owner was the *son* of the old owner?"

"Is. This wife of son."

We watched as she teetered across the grounds and came to a stop in front of us. "I have some things I need you to carry," she said.

I couldn't help but notice her hands. Each finger had a large gold ring, and the fingernails were impossibly long. How could she do anything with nails that long?

I was taken aback when I glanced up and realized she was

staring directly at me. I looked away.

"And are these your little campers?" she asked.

"We're here for the camp," Samantha said.

"Yeah, this is so cool," Danny added.

The woman chuckled—a kind of self-satisfied, superior little chuckle—as if she found the whole thing amusing, or as if she were laughing at Danny, or maybe at all of us.

"So you've come to learn about animals," she said. "Is this all of them?"

Vladimir nodded.

"Four campers. Not exactly the rousing success you expected when you set this whole thing up, is it?"

So this camp was Vladimir's idea. That would explain the brochure. He must have written it himself.

"Sometimes things are a lot more complicated than they appear," she said, pointing one of her perfect nails at him.

There was something about this woman. From the first glimpse I had of her, I didn't like her. The closer she got, the stronger the feeling became. Now that she was opening her mouth, it got stronger with each word and raised eyebrow.

"I'm sure there'll be more campers later on in the summer," Nick said.

"Or next year for sure," I added. I wanted to support Vladimir and deflate her. "Once we tell all our friends how good it was, they'll want to come next year."

"Next year," she repeated softly. "We'll just have to see what next year brings now, won't we?" There was something about the way she said that, or maybe the look on her face, that bothered me. Then again, everything about her seemed to bother me.

"Regardless, I need some help carrying in my groceries and a few other items I bought. Vladimir, come and bring them into the house." She paused. "Actually, all of you can come and help," she added as she turned and we watched her walk away.

"She wants us to help carry groceries?" Samantha asked, sounding as if it were beneath her.

"You no have to come," Vladimir said. "You go back and unpack and—"

"I'll help," Nick said.

"You?" I questioned. "You want to help carry groceries?" He never wanted to help with anything at home.

"No big deal. The sooner the job is done, the sooner Vladimir can get us to the elephant. Let's all go and help. How long can it take, anyway?"

I shrugged. "Whatever. We might as well help."

We started after her. It was kind of funny walking behind her, watching her move. It wasn't just that she kept wobbling and tottering on her heels, but she was weaving a strange route, trying to avoid the mud and the puddles that occupied the parts of the path not filled with gravel. Soon we were right beside her.

"So you four children are interested in animals," she said.

"Isn't everybody?" Danny answered.

"Not everybody...at least judging from the number of campers we have," she said, casting another look at Vladimir.

We came up to the big house. Sitting in front of it was an expensive sports utility vehicle.

"The bags are in the back seat and the trunk," she said, passing her keys over to Vladimir and heading into the house. If she was heading that way, why didn't she at least bring something in with her?

Nick opened the side door while Vladimir inserted the key and popped the trunk. The whole trunk was filled with bags. Some of them were plastic grocery bags while others—most of the others—didn't involve food. They held shoe boxes or had tissue paper sticking out and looked as if they had clothes in them

"Boss's wife like shop," Vladimir said as he hoisted some of the bags.

"Does she ever," I agreed. There were two dozen bags from

a variety of stores, and the name SMALL CAPS GRANVILLE'S was written in fancy lettering on the side of almost half of them. "It looks like she went on a shopping spree."

"Spree? What mean spree?"

"It means she spent a lot of money on a whole lot of things," I said.

"*Da*, she always doing spree. Clothes, lots of clothes, and shoes...many, many shoes."

"Are any of them good for walking on gravel paths?" I asked.

Vladimir smiled and shook his head.

We all grabbed bags and shuffled up the walk, following Vladimir to the side of the house and an open door. We entered and found ourselves in a new, modern kitchen. She was standing by the counter, pouring herself a mineral water.

"This is beautiful," I said.

"Yes, it is," she said smugly. "It lacks only one thing."

I looked around. I couldn't see anything missing.

"It lacks somebody to cook for us. I hate cooking."

"Sarah's a good cook," Nick said.

"Is she?" the woman asked. "Which one of you is Sarah?"

"Me. I'm Sarah. And this is my brother, Nick, and this is Samantha and her brother, Danny."

She nodded in their direction, a little smile on her face, as they mumbled greetings.

"Is the whole house this fancy?" Samantha asked.

Her smile became bigger, but no less phony. "The best of everything. My husband insists upon it." She paused. "Would you like a tour?"

"Sure, that would be nice!" Samantha said enthusiastically.

She actually reminded me of a smaller version of this woman.

"You can put the grocery bags right here on the counter. The other bags can come along with us, and you can leave them in my room."

We sorted out the bags, leaving some where she'd directed

and carrying the others.

"Before we start, I want everybody to take off their shoes and leave them in the kitchen. There's no way I want muddy footprints all over my beautiful new white carpet." She paused again. "By the way, my name is Krystal, with a *K*, but I suppose it would be best if you all called me Mrs. Armstrong, since I am the *owner*."

We trailed behind her from room to room. With each passing room, a number of things became more apparent. First, it was a really fancy home; second, everything in it was new and expensive; third, the only thing she liked better than her fancy things was herself; and fourth, I really, really, *really* didn't like her.

"And, finally, we'll end our tour with the entertainment room," she said, opening the door with a flourish.

I walked in a few steps and stopped. The entire far wall was taken up by the biggest TV I'd ever seen in my life. A baseball game—the players so big they were almost life-size—was on.

"That is...that is...amazing," Nick gasped.

A black leather chair spun around to face us. There was a man sitting in it. In one hand he held a drink, and in the other was a television converter. He pushed a button, and the TV became mute, while the action continued behind him. He was sitting at a desk, a computer alive beside him.

"Hello, Pooky!" she sang out as she rushed across the room and threw her arms around his neck. "Just wait until you see the things I bought today! You're going to love them!"

"I'm sure I will," he said. When he pushed another button, the gigantic screen clicked, darkened, and faded away to black.

"These must be our campers," he said as he rose from the chair and came toward us. He circled us, staring, his head cocked to one side, a hand on his chin, as if he was inspecting us. "Is this all of them?"

"That's all for the first week," Mrs. Armstrong said.

"I guess some ideas work out better than others," he said. "Hopefully you'll all have a good week. Apparently Vladimir knows all sorts of things about animals."

"But not as much as your father," Danny said.

"And how would you know that?" Mr. Armstrong asked.

"Vladimir told us about him."

"Yes, I've been told many stories myself. They say he always had time for an injured animal. Shame the same couldn't be said about people. By the way, Vladimir, how are those lion cubs doing?"

"Doing good."

"Excellent. That's great news!"

It was nice that he was interested in the animals—

"I've already received bids for all of them," he continued.

"Bids? You mean like in selling them?" I asked.

"Of course. I had three more e-mail offers today."

"But why are you selling them?" Nick asked.

"It takes a great deal of money to raise, feed, and maintain animals, especially large animals," he said.

There was enough money spent on those packages we had carried in to feed the whole park for a month.

"And you simply can't keep every animal that's born or your space would be overrun in no time," he continued.

I thought about all the empty pens in the park. There was lots of space still to be filled before there was any danger of them being "overrun."

"Will the cubs be ready to go in two weeks?" Mr. Armstrong asked.

Vladimir shrugged in response.

"Because their value goes down pretty fast as they get older. Do you kids have any idea what a baby lion is going for on the market these days?" He paused. "Come to think of it, that's none of your business." He turned back to the TV, clicking the game on again. The sound blasted out at us.

Mrs. Armstrong motioned us to the door and we exited. She closed the door behind us.

❧

"Did you hear that?" Nick asked, his voice cutting through the darkness of the cabin where we all lay in our beds.

"It would be hard to miss," I answered back.

"What was it?" Danny asked.

"Maybe a lion," Samantha replied.

"Nope, not a lion. More like a jaguar or a leopard," Nick disagreed.

Both the jaguars and the leopards weren't too far from our cabin. What a strange thought. We were going to go to sleep almost within sight, and definitely within sound, of more than two dozen types of different animals. It was weird, but kind of wonderful.

The call came once again. It was somehow high-pitched and growly at the same time. I had no idea what it was. It could have been aliens for all I knew. What I did know was that lying here in the dark with the different animal noises coming in through the open window was keeping me awake. Not that I would have necessarily been able to sleep even if it was completely quiet. There was just too much to think about—or as my mother said, to "process."

Aside from the new sights, the animals, and sleeping in this new place all squished up with three other kids, I was trying to figure out Vladimir and Mr. and Mrs. Armstrong.

Vladimir reminded me of some of the animals we'd seen: big, playful, and sort of friendly, rubbing against the bars and licking our hands. Still, they had long claws and sharp teeth, and a lick could become a bite pretty quick—a bite that could take off a finger, a hand, or even an arm. I liked Vladimir, or at least I thought I liked him, but there were things going on with him, things under the surface, that troubled me. Maybe even scared me a little.

Mr. and Mrs. Armstrong were different. I had no mixed feelings about them. I just didn't like them. I couldn't imagine two people owning an exotic animal park that were so uninterested in the animals. It was like somebody who was allergic to sugar and chocolate who owned a candy store. Why were they here if they didn't like animals? They couldn't be making a fortune doing this, or could they? It certainly looked as if they were spending a fortune. I figured we'd find out more tomorrow when the park officially opened for business and we saw how many people came through to look at the animals. Maybe at a few bucks a person it all added up to enough money to pay for that new house and all the things that were in it. Tonight, though, all I wanted to do was go to sleep and—

"Anybody know any scary stories?" Danny asked.

"I know a really scary one," I said.

"You do?" Nick asked.

"Sure," I said, "It's about this girl. Her name was Sarah, and nobody would let her sleep. So she got up in the middle of the night and strangled her little brother and some other little kid. I think his name was Danny. Want to hear it?" I asked.

"Not me," Danny said quietly. "I have to get to sleep."

"Good choice, and good night."

Chapter 6

"Come on, Sarah, nobody here cares how your hair looks," Nick said. "Actually, come to think of it, nobody *anywhere* cares how your hair looks."

I shot him a dirty look.

"Vladimir's waiting, and I want to get started this morning," Nick protested.

"I'm done," I said as I finished tying my hair into a ponytail.

Vladimir was outside standing beside the other kids.

"So, can we start off by getting a look at the baby lions?" Samantha asked.

"Or maybe riding the elephant?" Nick suggested.

Vladimir snorted. "No time for play till work done."

"What sort of work?" Nick asked.

"Give animals fresh water, clean pens, give food."

"Feeding them would be cool," Nick said. "I can do that."

"No. Nicki and Danny give water."

"And me?" Samantha asked. "What will I be doing?"

"You and big girl Sarah will work on food."

"Great, we get to feed them," she said, a taunting quality in her voice.

"That's not fair!" Danny said.

"Maybe you can do the food tomorrow," I offered.

"Let's get going," Samantha said.

"First show boys job and then show girls."

We trailed after Vladimir as he showed the boys their job. He gave them both a couple of watering cans. They were just like the type you would use to water plants, although they had very long necks. That was important, because while the water bowls for each animal obviously had to be inside the pen, the boys could add water from the outside. That was important to me. I needed to know they would be safe before I felt free to leave them.

Each time, before adding the water, the boys had to reach inside with a long-handled scrub brush and give the bowl a good scour. That way they didn't add good water to bad.

The first water delivery was to the two leopards. The cats, despite Nick's efforts to coax them closer, sat in the far corner of the pen, ignoring everybody. As we walked away, I noticed the leopards were already lapping up the fresh water.

The next animal was a jaguar. He, too, started off in the far corner, but as soon as Vladimir and the boys crossed behind the spectators' chain, he started to move. Slowly, going from behind one piece of cover to the next, he came toward them. It was obvious he was stalking them. Finally he made a tremendous rush for the fence and bounced against the mesh..

Nick, Danny, and their water containers flew into the air, and Vladimir burst into laughter. Once I was sure they were all safe, I had to admit I thought it was pretty funny, too.

Vladimir walked over to where we stood, and the boys followed. He was still chuckling. "Rest animals no problem. Boys keep give water. I show girls job."

We followed Vladimir into a small building. A big freezer, sort of like a meat locker, was on the far wall. On the other side there was a sink, a counter, and a big chopping block. The place was like a big, run-down kitchen.

"What's with all the flies?" Samantha asked.

That was a good question. They were buzzing through the air, and there must have been about a dozen fly strips covered with flies hanging from different places around the room.

"Flies like food. Food kept here. Big girl Sarah, brother say you like cooking."

"I think it's more that he likes me cooking so he can eat."

Vladimir chuckled again. "Funny joke. Girls fix food for animals."

"We're going to cook something for the animals?" Samantha asked.

"Not cook. Fix. I show."

Vladimir opened the door of the big meat locker. A frosty fog escaped the freezer as he walked inside. He grabbed a large container, walked out, and pushed the door closed with his foot, dropping the container onto the floor with a thud.

"Animals eat chicken," he said, taking off the lid to reveal the contents. It was filled with chickens—still covered with feathers. He reached in and grabbed one by the neck. Its lifeless limbs were still attached. "But before feed, must fix."

Vladimir dropped the bird onto the chopping block, grabbed a large cleaver with one hand, and brought it down with a resounding thud, cutting the head off the chicken. Samantha screamed and I shuddered. Quickly he spun the bird around and chopped off both feet, stretched out one wing, cut it off, and then did the same with the second wing.

"Next must take care of feathers," he said. With one hand he held the chicken, while with the second he started to rip out feathers. They came away from the flesh with a soft, ripping noise, like the sound made when you undo Velcro. "This bird ready," he said as he tossed it into the sink.

"You want us to give that bird to an animal?" Samantha asked.

"That bird and all rest. Need forty chickens. Here," he said, holding out the cleaver.

"You want us to do that?" Samantha asked in total disbelief.

Vladimir nodded.

"There's no way in the whole world I'm ever going to do that!" Samantha exclaimed. "Never!"

Vladimir looked confused. "Little girl Samantha not eat chicken?"

"Of course I eat chicken. I just never—"

"Give me the thing," I said, walking over and shaking my head. I took the cleaver from his hand. I was amazed at how heavy it was. Vladimir took out another chicken and plopped it onto the chopping block in front of me. Suddenly this didn't seem like such a good idea. I eyed the chicken. Its lifeless form looked back at me...the head tilted on a strange angle. It could have been sleeping. I really, really didn't want to do this. I glanced over at Samantha. She looked completely disgusted. Smiling, I brought the cleaver down with a resounding smack, cutting right through the neck.

The first half-dozen were the hardest. After that it was just *chop, chop, chop, chop,* and the chicken was separated from its head, legs, and two wings. Samantha had gone from looking as if she were going to run out the door to actually being able to help. She'd noticed an old pair of work gloves on a window ledge and, after putting them on, had slowly, carefully, plucked one of the birds. She got faster with the second, and then faster again, and was now almost keeping up with me.

"These flies are driving me crazy," I said.

"They're disgusting. I wish there was something we could do about them."

"Let's finish up fast and wait for Vladimir outside," I said. Once we'd gotten started he'd left to check on the boys and do some other chores.

"This isn't what I thought I'd be doing here," Samantha said as she stripped away the feathers from another bird.

"Me, neither. I thought I'd be cuddling with baby animals."

"It sounds like that Mr. Armstrong doesn't keep the babies around long enough to cuddle with," she said.

"I guess it takes a lot of money to buy all the stuff they have. It has to come from somewhere. I wonder what a lion cub *is* worth."

"I don't know, but I do know that Mrs. Armstrong shops at some pretty expensive stores," Samantha said. "Did you see all those bags from Granville's? That's a really fancy place."

"You've shopped there?"

"Not the one in this town, but the one where I live. Haven't you ever been in one of their stores?"

She had that annoying "I'm better than you" tone to her voice again. "I've never even heard of it," I said. "So I doubt they've got a store near where I live."

"That's too bad because—"

"Chicken all ready?" Vladimir asked as he came back in through the door.

"Almost," I said, grateful for the interruption. "Just a couple more to do. How are the boys doing?"

"Doing good. Finish with water. Now cleaning pen."

"Which pen?" I asked in alarm.

"Kushna...tiger."

"But you said he was dangerous!"

"Is, but boys safe. Lock Kushna in side pen. Big girl Sarah worry too much. Vladimir take care everything. Everything good. Come, feed animals."

We followed Vladimir across the compound. He was pushing a wheelbarrow filled with the chickens we'd prepared.

"Look, goats!" Samantha said.

There were five or six wandering around.

"Do you want us to catch them?" I asked.

"No catch. Let goats go free in park each morning. Goats, duckies, chickens, pheasants go free during day and put away at night in pen."

"Why do you put them away at night?" I asked.

"Keep safe."

"Safe from what?"

"Coyotes."

"I didn't know you had coyotes," I said.

"Vladimir not have. Nature has. Coyotes live in forest and come into park at night sometimes to eat from garbage cans."

"And they'd eat the goats?" I asked. Those goats were a fair size and had horns. They looked as if they could take care of themselves.

"Wouldn't it be easier to keep the goats and other animals in cages all the time?" Samantha asked.

"Easier, but visitors like to pet animals."

"Speaking of visitors, when does the park open?" I asked.

Vladimir looked at his watch. "Park open ten minutes ago."

I looked around. Other than us and the goats I didn't see anybody else.

"Will be busy day today. Many groups of kids come to see animals."

The words were hardly out of his mouth when I caught sight of a bunch of kids coming along the path. They were all wearing red baseball caps and were led by a large woman sporting the same hat. As the path opened up, the kids spread out. Some stayed behind the leader, while others walked or ran off in different directions, peering into the various cages.

As that group dispersed, I saw more people heading up the path. There was an older couple, a family with three kids, and behind them another cluster of kids. Vladimir was right; it was going to get busy.

⁂

The boys were still inside the tiger's cage with a shovel, a rake, and a big garbage can. They'd been scooping up tiger poop, bones, and food scraps and putting them in the garbage can.

Kushna was locked into a little pen at the side of his cage. Vladimir said it was a "lock-out" pen. I hadn't noticed before he'd mentioned it, but there was one of those attached to every pen. It was where they put the animals when the big pen was cleaned or if they needed to have a closer look at the animal.

We moved around to the lock-out area to feed Kushna. As we walked, I watched the tiger. He was studying the boys as they cleaned his pen. His eyes were on them the whole time. Then Kushna caught sight of us coming up the side. He bounded over and stood straight up at the pen, reaching almost to the top of the mesh. Thank goodness it had a fenced roof, or he could have been over in a second. In the little cage he seemed even bigger, and scarier.

"Come give Vlady a big kiss!"

Kushna met Vladimir at the fence and rubbed against him.

"Give Kushna two chickens...push through hole," Vladimir said.

I took two of the birds and walked over to a small metal-ringed hole in the fence that was large enough to allow a chicken through. As I pushed the first chicken in, there was a *whoosh*, and Kushna bounced over and ripped the bird out of my hands. I stumbled back a step in shock.

"Kushna like chicken. Put in second birdie."

I looked down at the bird in my hand, over at Vladimir, and then at Kushna chomping on the first chicken.

"I think Samantha should give him this one," I said, offering it to her. "I wouldn't want to cheat her out of the chance to feed a tiger."

She didn't look too happy about the suggestion, but reluctantly came forward. She took the bird and pushed it through the hole. It dropped to the ground, almost hitting Kushna in the head as he crunched down on the other chicken.

"Is that all he gets to eat?" Samantha asked.

"Eats different type meat. Today eat chicken. Four chickens."

"But we only gave him two," I said.

"Two for breakfast. Get two more at lunch feeding. Feed other animals now."

We circled back to the front of the cage. I gave Nick a little wave.

"How's it going?" I yelled.

"We're almost finished!" Danny called back. "The pen's looking really good!"

"See you later!" I said, and they both waved back. "How often do you have to clean the pens?" I asked Vladimir.

"Clean when have chance. In old days try to clean every few days."

"But you don't clean them as often now?"

"No time since old boss go."

"I guess he'd help," Samantha said.

"Not just help. Others help, too."

"What others?" I asked. I hadn't seen anybody else helping out.

"Was other people. Help feed, clean pens...now nobody but Vladimir."

"You must have to work almost nonstop to keep up with everything," I said.

"Work all time, but not keep up. Always something to be done. Always pen that should be cleaned, or fence fixed, or animal need food or water or is sick and need be healed. Always something," he said, shaking his head. "Big girl Sarah, little girl Samantha, and boys big help to have for Vladimir. Big help."

"That's okay we're just glad to—"

"Hey, what you do!" Vladimir screamed.

He stomped off toward a boy about Nick's age who was standing in front of a pen. In his hand was a stick. Vladimir reached out and grabbed the stick from the boy. "What you think you do, poking animal!" he yelled.

"I...I...I," the boy stammered.

"You think fun to hurt animal?" Vladimir demanded. "How you like if Vladimir poke you with stick?"

The boy's mouth opened again, but no words came out.

"You nothing but mean boy. Fat mean boy!"

The boy certainly was a little chunky, but not fat, and even if he was, that wasn't a very nice thing to say.

"Maybe should put fat boy in cage with animal he tease. You like to be meal for jaguar, fat boy?"

"Muuuuummmmmy!" the boy screamed, turning and running away as fast as his legs would carry him.

"I don't think you should have done that," I said to Vladimir.

"No let boy hurt or tease animals."

"But what if his mother comes back?" Samantha asked.

"I tell she have mean, fat son and kick both out of park," he said with a laugh, and we chuckled along with him. I could picture him both saying those words and then doing it.

"Vladimir never let nobody hurt animals when Vladimir here." He'd said those last few words quietly, barely opening his mouth. His voice was soft, but the way he said the words was something completely different. He sounded threatening, menacing, scary once again. I knew I'd never want to get him mad at me.

Chapter 7

"Sarah, wake up!"

"Leave me alone," I mumbled as I pulled the covers over my head to block both my brother's voice and the bright sunlight. Sunlight...it was obviously morning, but how early in the morning?

"Come on, Sarah, you have to get up!"

"I don't have to do anything. What time is it?"

"It's after eight."

"In the morning?"

"Of course. Everybody else has been up for close to two hours. Come on right now or you'll miss everything!"

"The only thing I'm missing is my sleep. Leave me alone now—or else."

"Fine. No big problem for me," Nick said. "Vladimir told me to come and get you, and I tried. You already missed the first one being born, and now you'll miss the second one."

Being born? I pushed the covers off, sat up, and squinted as I tried to open my eyes. The room was brilliantly bright. Samantha's and Danny's beds were empty.

"Where are they?" I asked, pointing at the bunk beds.

"They're there already, and I'm going back."

"Hold on!" I yelled.

"You hold on. I'm not going to miss it."

"Just wait. Something was born?" I asked.

"A little deer. It was amazing! Vladimir said a second one's on the way. But we have to go now or we'll miss it!"

"But I'm not dressed and I have to wash up and—"

"Suit yourself. I'm going back right now."

"Wait!" I called out. "Let me just throw on a sweater and my shoes."

"Just hurry!"

I jumped out of bed, stumbling over the tangle of sheets and covers still wrapped around my feet, but recovered before I fell face first to the floor.

"Real graceful, Sarah."

I ignored him, grabbed a sweater from the top drawer of the dresser, and pulled it over my pajama top. The bottoms sort of looked like sweat pants, so I left them on. Slipping my feet into my running shoes, I figured I could tie them up later.

"I'm gone," Nick said as he disappeared out the door.

I hurried across the cabin, pulling the door closed behind me, leaped off the porch, and rushed after Nick, who was trotting away. "Wait up!"

"Hurry up!" he shouted over his shoulder.

I doubled my pace as I passed Boo Boo's cage. Glancing over, I saw the bear lying on her back. She looked as if she were sound asleep. Even the animals were still sleeping.

"How did you know something was being born?" I asked as I pulled alongside Nick.

"Vladimir woke us up. He thought it would be something we'd want to see."

"Why wasn't I woken up?"

"We tried. You just lay there snoring away—"

"I don't snore!" I protested.

"Yeah, right," Nick muttered. "You stopped snoring long enough to mumble that we should leave you alone, so we did."

"I don't remember any of that."

"That doesn't surprise me. It was as if you were talking in your sleep." Nick paused. "What time did you get to sleep last night?"

Nick knew me better than I liked. "I went to bed the same time as you."

"That wasn't what I asked. When did you get to sleep?"

"I'm not sure." That was at least an honest answer. I had no idea how long I'd been awake in the dark, tossing and turning.

Up ahead I caught sight of Samantha, Danny, and Vladimir. They were standing at the fence of the deer pen. It was one of the largest pens and contained the biggest collection of animals. It held dozens of deer as well as caribou and four gigantic buffalo— their thick winter coats hanging off them, making them look as if they were melting in the summer heat. Samantha had her video camera with her and was filming the pen.

"Have we missed it?" Nick questioned.

"No, it hasn't happened yet," Samantha answered, staring through the mesh.

"Did you get it on video?" I asked, hoping I could at least see it that way.

"Most of it."

"Which deer is having the—" I stopped mid-sentence as I caught sight of a deer, no more than three dozen feet away, crouching beside some bushes. At her side was a small bundle of wet fur. It was nuzzled up to her—maybe it was even nursing— and she was licking it. It was tiny, no bigger than a large cat.

"How long could this take?" Danny asked.

"Should be now," Vladimir said.

"Maybe she's only having one baby," I suggested.

"Not one. Two. Having two babies."

"It was amazing seeing the first one," Samantha said. "You should have seen it!"

Even when she didn't mean it, her voice always had that "na-na-na-na" quality to it, as if she was one up on you.

"It was something," Danny agreed.

"The deer was just standing there, chewing on some grass, and then this little wet bundle of fur dropped out," Nick said. "I couldn't believe—"

"Look!" Danny shouted, pointing through the fence.

The baby deer was struggling to its feet. On pencil-thin, spindly legs, it tottered and wobbled a few steps.

"It's only fifteen minutes old, and it took its first steps. That deer's a genius!" Nick declared.

"All animals have to walk right away, or they'll be killed by wolves or something," I said.

"But that fast?" Nick questioned. "I'm telling you, it's an advanced deer."

"Nope, I'm certain," I said. "Right, Vladimir?"

He didn't answer. He was staring at the mother deer. She had rolled onto her side, as if she was resting.

"Baby deer walk really soon, right, Vladimir?" I asked.

"Not good," he muttered.

"Not good? It shouldn't be walking?"

"Should be standing."

"It is standing. It's walking!" Nick said.

"Not baby. Mummy deer. Should be standing."

"Maybe she's just resting," I suggested. "She must be tired."

Vladimir shook his head. "Bad. Very bad. Can't give birth on side. Baby not coming right. Maybe die."

"The baby's going to die?" Samantha exclaimed. "Can't you do something?"

"Can, but need help."

"We can help!" Nick said.

"Yeah, we can," Samantha agreed as Danny nodded enthusiastically.

I wasn't so sure—what did he mean by help?

"Come, follow," Vladimir said.

He raced around the side of the pen, and we hurried after him. Stopping at the entrance, Vladimir pulled out a large set of keys from his pocket. He fumbled with them until he found the right one, then inserted it into the big padlock that secured the chain, holding the gate closed. "Nick, Danny, grab shovel and rake."

"What?" Nick asked.

"Shovel, rake," he said, pointing at the two tools leaning against the fence. "Grab, take."

"You want them to clean the cage now?" I asked in amazement.

"Not clean cage. Just do as told," Vladimir ordered.

Nick picked up both and handed Danny the rake as Vladimir swung open the gate and motioned for us to follow. I hesitated for a split second before I entered, thinking about that first time I entered Buddha's pen. Of course, this was different. This wasn't like going in with a tiger. It was going in with animals that a tiger would eat.

Vladimir pulled the gate shut and then took the chain and wrapped it around, finally clicking the lock back into place and sealing us in. I guess he wanted to make sure nothing got out.

"Move slow, quiet like little mouses," Vladimir said.

That made sense. We didn't want to spook any of the animals, especially the mother deer or the baby.

"What are the shovel and rake for?" Nick whispered.

"Protect."

"Protect from what?"

"We try to help deer. Deer not know. Buffalo not care. Can charge or trample."

I'd forgotten all about the buffalo. I looked anxiously at the far end of the pen where the four big animals were grazing.

"How will a shovel protect us?" I asked.

"Wave in air and chase animals away."

"That will scare them?" Nick asked.

"Maybe," Vladimir said.

"Maybe? You don't know?"

"Never try," he said with a shrug.

That wasn't the reassurance I was looking for.

As we continued to advance, I noticed how most of the animals were moving around us, squeezing to the fence and then heading for the far end of the pen to put as much space as possible between us and them.

Vladimir motioned for us to spread out. Danny and his rake moved to one side, while Nick and his shovel took up the far side. The animals continued to move by us. They seemed more afraid of us than we were of them. That was good. I wasn't counting too heavily on my brother and his shovel to protect me from a charging animal.

Up ahead the mother deer continued to lie on her side. The little baby, still standing beside her on his little legs, was nursing. What was going to happen when we got closer? Would she run and leave the baby, or would she charge to protect it from us? Either way wouldn't be any good. If she ran, we couldn't help her, and if she charged, we couldn't even help ourselves.

Vladimir slowed his pace and we did the same, maintaining a line across the narrowing end of the pen. The deer still didn't move. Didn't she notice us...didn't she care...or couldn't she move? That last thought sent a chill up my spine. The deer turned her head and looked at us, but still she didn't move.

"Nicolai, Danny, stop, turn round. Watch if animals come."

"And if they do?" Danny asked.

"Wave rake in the air, jump up, jump down, yell words. Act like crazy person. Animals much 'fraid of crazy man. Girls, come," Vladimir said, motioning us to follow.

We did as he said until we were standing right over top of the deer. She looked up at us with those big brown, soft, liquid, eyes. She seemed afraid. No, not just afraid—as if she was in pain.

Vladimir bent down and ran his hand along the side of the deer.

"What is it?" Samantha asked.

"Baby coming out wrong. All twisted around, caught up inside. Feet and legs all pointing out different ways. Feet coming out first. Can't come out first—breach birth."

"You said we could do something," Samantha said.

"We try. Girls, come, must hold deer."

"Hold the deer?" I asked.

"*Da*. Must hold deer, talk to deer."

"How will that help?"

"Will keep deer calm while I turn baby around."

"How do you turn the baby around?" I asked.

"Reach inside and twist."

Samantha's surprised expression reflected my shock.

"You're joking—right?" I said.

"No joke. If no turn, then mummy deer die, baby deer die. Have to," he said as he started to roll up the sleeve of his right arm, "hold deer."

I dropped to my knees, as did Samantha. Gently I moved aside the little baby deer with my hands. It was as light as a feather and shifted to allow me in. The mother deer's side moved up and down with each strained breath. It wasn't regular, but seemed to be coming in starts and stops. I stroked the deer. She was warm, soft, and smooth.

Looking up, I saw Samantha cradling the deer's head. She was talking, actually whispering something. I couldn't hear what she was saying, but the tone of her voice was gentle and soothing. It even made me feel calmer. Maybe she wasn't as annoying as I had thought.

"Hold tight," Vladimir said.

I tried to strengthen my grip. It was hard. My arms didn't even come close to spanning the width of the deer, and I knew that if she chose to struggle to her feet, I would be hopeless to restrain her.

"It's going to be okay, girl," Samantha said, and for an instant I thought she was talking to me.

I looked up at Samantha. She was probably just as scared as I was, but she didn't appear to be. She seemed calm, almost brave. The deer shuddered violently, and I fought the urge to let go and run. Instead I held on tighter.

"As thought," Vladimir puffed. "Baby wrong way. I turn."

I moved so that I was facing away from him. I could only hope he could do it. The deer shook, strained, and jerked. Was she trying to get to her feet? I pressed my whole body against the deer, wrapping my arms around her as far as I could, pressing my face into her side, all of my weight trying to hold her in place. The deer jerked again—Vladimir had to hurry. This couldn't go on much longer or we wouldn't be able to—

"Baby okay!" Vladimir screamed.

"She's okay!" I yelled, letting go of my grip and looking up. Vladimir was holding a small bundle of wet, goopy, brown fur. Staring out were two brown eyes—it had its mother's eyes!

"Here, Sarah, hold baby," he said, thrusting the creature forward into my arms.

It was a wet, warm ball, and I pulled it close to me. We'd done it. We'd saved the little deer's life. I felt like laughing, crying, screaming, or something.

"Look at all the people," Samantha said.

"People, what—" I started to say when I caught sight of a crowd standing outside the fence, watching. There must have been twenty, thirty, or more of them. "Where did they come from?" I gasped.

"Park open. Tourists. Sarah, take baby, Samantha take other baby. We have to go."

"But won't the mother get angry if we take away her babies?" I asked.

Vladimir shook his head. "Mother no get anything. Mummy deer is dead."

Chapter 8

I felt all the blood drain from my face. "She's...she's..."

"Dead," Vladimir said softly.

I turned away from him to stare at the deer. Her head, still cradled in Samantha's arms, was limp. The eyes were open—still brown, but now different, not just unmoving and lifeless, but almost peaceful.

"How did it happen?" I gasped.

"Lose blood. Too much blood gone to live."

I looked down at the little baby wiggling in my arms. Its fur was slicked back, soaked. Was it blood? My top was stained where the baby deer had pressed against me, and my hands and arms were covered, as well.

My eyes fell on Vladimir. He was covered in blood from the tips of his fingers, up his arms, his shirt, and pants. At his feet was a large puddle of liquid.

"How did this happen?" I asked, my voice barely a whisper, "Couldn't we have done something?"

Vladimir shook his head sadly. "Nothing."

"What if we had called a veterinarian?" Samantha asked.

"No. Could not help. Even old boss could not save deer."

"Maybe we should have just left it alone," she said.

"Leave alone, then both mother and baby die. We help and

little one able to live. We do right."

My chin started to quiver, and my tongue felt as if it were getting thick. I knew that tears were close, but I didn't want to cry. I bit down on the inside of my cheek to force the tears back.

The little deer moved in my arms. I pulled it closer. Poor baby. Poor motherless baby. Who would take care of it? How would it live without its mother? All of a sudden the tears exploded from my eyes. Almost at the same instant, Samantha began to bawl.

"Stop crying!" Vladimir barked. "Stop now!"

How could we not cry?

"You want babies to die, too?" he demanded.

"Babies? The baby deer might die?" I sobbed.

"Not might, *will* die unless we do things. No time to cry. Time to do."

"What do we have to do?" I asked, sniffling back the tears.

"Come, bring deer."

Vladimir stood up, swept the other baby deer into his arms, and handed it to Samantha, who had released her grip on the mother deer and taken to her feet, as well. I struggled to get up, and Vladimir reached down and grabbed me by the shoulders, helping me to stand.

"Must go quick," he said.

Carefully Samantha and I started after Vladimir, who had already passed Nick and Danny. I wanted to move quickly but was afraid of tripping and falling on the little deer, or dropping it. I had to be careful.

Moving in the direction of the gate now, we were walking straight toward the other animals. The deer seemed to be watching us, as if they were wondering why we were carrying the babies, or perhaps they were thinking we were responsible for the death of their mother. Thank goodness the buffalo seemed completely absorbed in eating and weren't even facing us.

I also couldn't help noticing how all along the outside of the fence the park visitors were following us, trying to get a better look at the babies.

"Hurry up!" Vladimir called. He was at the gate. He'd already unlocked it, removed the chain, and stood there with the gate wide open. Danny and Nick were by his side, along with a small crowd of people waiting just outside the fence.

Samantha and I moved more quickly. We reached them and exited through the gate while Vladimir secured it behind us.

"Take deer to Vladimir's house. Go in back door to kitchen. I meet you there."

Where are you going?" I demanded.

"No time to explain. Just go."

Vladimir moved effortlessly through the crowd. It wasn't just that he was so big that people got out of his way. Quite obviously nobody was interested in him. All they wanted to see was the newborn deer.

As I tried to move forward, the crowd closed in on me. People thrust their cameras at us, snapping pictures, and hands came out to touch the deer. We were bombarded by questions and comments. I could hardly move.

"Excuse me," I said.

People kept pressing forward, trying to see the babies. All I could hear was cooing and comments about how small and cute they were.

"Can I hold one of them?" somebody asked.

"No...you don't understand. We have to get going."

"Just let us take a few pictures—"

"Please leave them alone!" I screamed. "Leave us alone. Don't you understand? If you don't let us through, the deer will die!"

Suddenly there wasn't a sound, and everybody seemed to be staring at me instead of the deer.

"We have to take care of them right away," I gasped, embarrassed by my outburst as I stumbled forward and the crowd parted for us.

"I thought I was going to have to hit them with my shovel," Nick said as we left the crowd behind.

"So did I," I admitted.

We continued to pass people as we moved along the path. Their reactions were shock, surprise, and delight. We must have had another half-dozen pictures taken as people fumbled for their cameras. It was strange being the centre of everybody's attention—or at least *holding* something that was the centre of attention.

We circled around the side of Vladimir's house.

"Can you get the door?" I asked Danny.

He opened it and we went inside. We were standing in the middle of the kitchen.

"What now?" Samantha asked.

"We wait for Vladimir."

"Where did he go?" Nick asked.

"I don't know any more than you do." I paused. "I think you can put down the shovel now."

"I sort of forgot I was still holding it," he admitted, leaning it against the counter. "Do you think I could hold the deer instead?"

"Sure," I said as I offered it to him.

"Me, too!" Danny exclaimed.

"Okay, my arms were getting tired, anyway," Samantha said as she handed the baby to her brother.

"It's so light," Danny said as he took it into his arms.

"Not after you've been carrying it for a while," I said. "I just hope Vladimir gets here soon or else—"

"Have to wash deer, dry deer!" Vladimir yelled as he burst through the door. Under one arm he was carrying a pile of books and papers. He put them on the table and went straight to the sink.

"Must fill with warm water. Mummy deer would clean. We must clean," he said as he started to fill the sink with water.

"Big girl Sarah, you look at books and papers."

"What are they?" I asked.

"Animal books—to make food."

"Like a cookbook?" I asked.

"Cookbook?" Vladimir asked.

"Yeah, they contain recipes for food."

"*Da, da.* Those are cookbooks. We have to find recipe for deer."

"For the deer?" I gasped.

"To eat. Must eat."

"You can't!" I exclaimed. He wanted to eat the deer!

"We won't let you!" Samantha shouted as she stepped forward and put herself between Vladimir and the two babies in the arms of our brothers.

Vladimir turned from the sink and looked at us. He wore a look of total confusion. "But need to eat. Have to eat."

"We won't let you eat these deer!" Samantha yelled.

Good for her!

"No, no, not *eat* deers. Deers must *eat*," Vladimir said.

"You want to feed the deers?" I asked.

"*Da.* No mummy to feed, so we must feed." He paused and his brow furrowed. "You think I want to eat babies?"

"Well..." I muttered, looking at the floor.

"That is what you said," Samantha argued.

Vladimir's face got serious and scary, and then he began to laugh—big, loud, rolling laughter. "Vladimir here to protect animals, not eat. Come, bring deers."

Nick and Danny brought the deer to Vladimir, who gently placed first one and then the other in the sink.

"Hold little ones here, gentle like made glass."

While Nick and Danny again put their hands on the deer, Vladimir turned on the taps and filled the sink with water. He tested the water, adjusting first the hot and then the cold water.

"Mummy deer would lick clean. We scrub."

"I think this one likes the water," Nick said.

"Mine, too," Danny added.

"Big girl Sarah, you go through books. Find page tell what feed deer."

I looked at the stack of notebooks and loose pages. "Where should I start?"

"Start top, go bottom."

"But that could take all day."

"Not have all day. Quit talk, start look."

"But don't you have any idea where to look?" I asked.

"*Da.* Look in books."

"Couldn't you help me?" I pleaded. Surely he'd have a better idea than me where to look, or would recognize it when he saw it.

"Vladimir wash deer. 'Sides, no can read."

"You can't read?" Nick asked in amazement.

"Can read. Can't read English. Can read Russian and Polish and some Latvian. Even read some English, but not good. How many languages can Nicolai read?"

"Um...just one."

I chuckled. "And not even very well in that one."

"Shut up, Sarah!"

"No tell big girl sister Sarah to shut up. Should always respect big sister."

Nick looked as if he wanted to say something back, but I figured the thought of respecting me had caught him so off guard he didn't know what to say.

"Books made by old boss. He make lots of notes about animals. Lots of things like how to make sick buffalo better, or fixing broken wing of bird, what vitamins to add and what to feed animals."

"Baby deer?" I asked.

"Like deer," he said.

"Do you want me to help look?" Samantha offered.

"No, you have job to do. Find towels to dry babies after bath."

"How about if we blow-dry them?" Samantha offered.

"No have blow dryer."

"I do," Samantha said.

"I brought one, too," I said. "Would those work?"

"Work good. Go and get."

Samantha raced out the door, and I flipped open the cover of the first notebook. In messy handwriting was an index. I scanned the page. It listed things like "A lion had a belly ache," "Raccoon chow," and "Shoes for a sore-footed sloth." If I had time, I would have liked to have read through those. Maybe I could look at them later.

I closed the first notebook and grabbed the second. This one was even messier, the handwriting shaky and hard to read, and there was no index at the front. I'd have to go through it page by page.

I couldn't help but glance up at the action at the sink. My view was partially blocked by the backs of the boys and Vladimir, but I could still see the little deer. They were standing in the water in the sink, and everything except their eyes was covered by thick white suds and lather. They looked cute and silly at the same time.

Vladimir picked up a plastic cup from the counter, dipped it in the water, and poured it over the head of one of the deer. The suds melted away with the water, revealing a shiny brown coat punctuated by tiny white markings that hadn't been visible before.

"I got them!" Samantha yelled as she charged through the doorway holding a blow dryer in each hand.

"Good, good. Almost finished washing. Just getting off soap. Big girl, Sarah, have you found food?"

"I'm still looking," I said, flipping the pages again. "There's a lot of information in here and I—I found it!" I jumped up from the kitchen table and brought the book over so everybody could see. "It says you can use cow's milk, homogenized, and then add some cream to it to make it even richer. It should be heated to match the temperature of a deer, but it doesn't say what temperature that is."

"I know temperature," Vladimir said. "It say more?"

"Yeah, it says to add vitamins, some liquid vitamins."

"Probably vitamin D and maybe iron," Vladimir said.

"That's exactly what it says."

Vladimir smiled. "Got lots of vitamins in feed shed."

"And then... This is strange."

"What?" Samantha asked.

"It says we're supposed to use a glove to feed them."

"A glove?" Samantha blurted. "You're kidding, right?"

"No, that's what it says. There's even a picture," I said, tilting the picture toward her. It showed three crudely drawn little deer each suckling a different finger of a glove. The other end, the place where the hand would go, held a big bottle, and it looked as if it was secured by a big elastic band.

"I think it's some sort of rubber glove with holes cut in the end," I said. "Do you have something like that around?"

Vladimir shook his head. "But I have bottles we could use and—wait, I see boss's wife use gloves to wash dishes. Maybe we can take old pair."

"Do you think she'd mind?" I questioned.

"Maybe, maybe not," Vladimir said, shrugging. "Big girl Sarah, you go and ask."

"Me? Why me?"

"Other kids dry deer. Vladimir mix food for deer."

"But wouldn't it be better if you were the one who asked?"

Vladimir snickered. "Better if big girl Sarah ask. Better if anybody instead of Vladimir ask. You go."

"Could Samantha come with me?"

"Sure, I could go along with—"

"No," Vladimir barked, cutting her off. "Little girl stay to read words from book so Vladimir can fix food."

I opened my mouth to argue, but closed it again. As much as I didn't really want to go, either alone or with somebody, I was quickly learning that there was no point in arguing with Vladimir. Maybe he didn't look like my mother, but they did have that in common.

"Hurry," Vladimir said, shooing me.

I handed the book to Samantha and started for the door.

"And no go front door of house. Go side, kitchen—*servant* entrance."

I knocked on the door again. There was still no answer. I knocked a third time, much louder, so loud that the window rattled ominously and there was no doubt it could be heard in the entire house. That was assuming somebody was home. I waited and listened, holding my breath, my head turned, an ear almost touching the door. I didn't have time to wait for them to answer the door. Maybe they were still in bed. If they had been asleep, that knock would have woken the dead. Maybe they weren't home.

I looked up the driveway. The garage door was open. The big new SUV, which I had helped unload yesterday, was nowhere to be seen. They must be out, and I certainly didn't have time to wait for them to get back. Then again, maybe I didn't have to wait.

I put a hand on the doorknob and tentatively turned it. It wasn't locked. Slowly I pushed the door, and it swung open silently to reveal an empty kitchen.

"Hello!" I called out.

Nothing. I leaned in, my head over the threshold but my feet still firmly planted outside. Craning my head, I could see the whole kitchen. There was nobody. I took a small half step into the kitchen. Part of me was screaming that I shouldn't be walking into somebody's house, but the other half was just as sure I had no choice. I had to do it for the babies. That half won the internal argument, and I moved forward.

There were a few dirty dishes on the counter, the table had two place settings, already used for breakfast, and the sink was half-filled with dirty water. I didn't see any gloves. Not on the counter nor draped over the tap—that was where my mother always put our rubber gloves. If they weren't visible on the counter, then maybe they were under the counter.

I dropped to my knees and opened the twin cupboard doors under the sink. There was an amazing assortment of bottles and jars—mostly unopened cleaning products—partially folded plastic grocery bags, and a scrubbing brush, but no gloves. I moved aside a big bottle of bleach so I could see the back of the cupboard. There, in the very back, hanging up with clothes-pins, were two pairs of gloves! I reached in to grab them.

"Looking for something?"

I jumped up, smashing my head on the top of the cupboard.

"Oww!" I screamed as I scrambled to my feet, one hand holding the gloves while the other went to the spot on my head where I'd hit. Mr. Armstrong was standing in front of me.

"Looking for something?" he repeated.

"I found them," I said, holding up the gloves.

"You broke into our house to wash the dishes?"

"I didn't break in, honestly," I pleaded. "The door wasn't locked."

"Probably wasn't locked, but certainly not wide open," he said, gesturing to the gaping door. "Is it common practice where you come from to just walk into somebody's house?"

"I knocked first."

"I heard you."

"You did? But if you heard me knocking then..."

"Why didn't I answer?" he asked, completing my sentence.

I nodded.

"I was on the Internet conducting some business, and I thought my wife would get it. I didn't realize she'd already left. She's out shopping again."

"I'm really sorry. I wouldn't have walked in like that, but Vladimir told me to come and—"

"And just walk into our house?" he demanded. For the first time his tone seemed angry.

"No, no, he just said I should come and ask for—"

"I'm surprised he'd have you *ask* for anything. He doesn't seem to understand that I own the park and he is just an employee. He walks around here like he's the owner!"

"He told me to go to the back door, knock, and ask if we could have a glove," I said, trying to defend Vladimir.

"One of my father's faults, and believe me he had many, was that he treated these animals and his employees like they were family." He paused, and a scowl creased his face. "No, that's wrong. He didn't treat them like family. He treated them like he *should* have treated his family, but didn't."

I didn't know what to say to that.

"I wouldn't have come in at all unless it was an emergency."

"A dish-washing emergency?" he asked incredulously.

"No, a deer-feeding emergency. We needed the glove to feed the newborn deer."

"There's a new deer?"

"Two of them."

"I wasn't informed of any new births."

"It just happened less than an hour ago."

He nodded. "I still don't understand what a glove has to do with any of that."

"It's to feed them. They suckle off the fingers of the glove."

"That certainly sounds like another one of Vladimir's, shall we say, *interesting* ideas."

"It's not Vladimir's idea," I said. "It's your father's."

"My father?"

"I read it in one of his notebooks. He wrote about feeding

newborn deer. So, could I have a glove, or maybe even a pair of them?"

He shook his head and let out a deep sigh. "That would be all right, I imagine."

"Thanks." I put the yellow pair down on the counter, holding on to the pink ones. I didn't know if deer could see in colour, but if they could, these were a closer match to their mother's udder than the yellow pair. "I better get going. The sooner they eat the better."

"That would be wise. We wouldn't want anything to happen to those babies."

For a split second his comment caught me off guard. Maybe there was more of his father in him than I'd given him credit for.

"Because a live deer is certainly worth much more than a dead one," he continued. "I wonder how much a petting zoo would pay for a pair of baby deer."

"But they can't go anywhere. They're too young!" I protested.

"They certainly are now. But in a few weeks..." He paused, and a thoughtful look crossed his face. "Maybe I should make a few calls and get on the Internet right now to find out who might be interested and at what price. Close the door on your way out."

"Settle down!" I said loudly as the two babies scrambled and pushed against each other, hungrily suckling on the glove. They'd already drained the contents of two whole bottles and were still going at it with reckless abandon. "Come on, guys, there's enough room and milk for everybody."

"I can't get over how hungry they are," Nick said.

"If not hungry, not live," Vladimir said.

"But why do they have to fight each other?" I asked.

"Fighting for life. Sometimes strong deer live and weak one die."

"But both of these will live—right?" I asked.

Vladimir reached over and ran his hands over one deer. He then lifted it while its mouth remained locked on the tip of one of the fingers of the glove, then did the same thing to the second baby. "Babies look strong, feed good, should live—both."

"Could I feed them now?" Danny asked.

"Sure, no problem," I said as I struggled to my feet.

"No!" Vladimir said, holding up his hands. "Big girl Sarah feed them."

"That's okay. I've had a turn."

"Feeding not for kids. Feeding for deer. One mummy feed. Big girl Sarah is mummy to deer."

"Sarah's their mother?" Nick questioned.

"*Da.* Watch. Pull glove away from deer."

"But they're still so—" I started to protest, but stopped myself.

Gently I pulled the glove, pushing them away with my free hand. They both stood on their back legs, reaching up, trying to get the glove as I pulled it free.

"Now put on table where deer can't get," Vladimir said.

I put it down.

"Now walk to door," he ordered.

I didn't understand why, but I listened. The little deer bounced against the backs of my legs as I moved. I stopped, and they both rubbed against me, looking up at me with those beautiful brown eyes.

"Go into other room and then come back," Vladimir said.

I walked out of the room and the two babies bounced along with me. When I turned around and came back, they were right there by my feet, like two little shadows.

"Congratulations, big girl Sarah, you mother!"

Chapter 9

I jumped slightly up and my eyes popped open as the cold, wet little nose pressed against my face. A second little nose attached to a second set of beautiful brown eyes pressed against me. I wanted to roll over and pull up the covers, but I knew I had to feed the baby deer. A little tongue shot out and licked my face. I guess I should have found it cute—and really it was—but it had become less cute each time it happened. Every hour and a half all through the night I'd fed them, and this was the sixth or seventh time

There was bright light streaming in through the windows. Obviously it was no longer night. I looked at the clock. Five thirty-seven. It was way too early to be awake. Across the room I could see Samantha still sound asleep. Although I couldn't see Danny in the bunk above her or Nick in the bed above me, I knew that neither of them would be awake.

One deer reared up on her hind legs and gave me a head butt in the face.

"Okay, okay, I'm getting up."

I climbed out of bed. On the dresser was the glove and bottle, ready to be filled with milk. Beside them sat three big thermos bottles. Two were empty, while the third was still half-filled. Vladimir had made a big batch of formula, heated it up, and poured it into the thermoses so I could feed the deer throughout the night. When he originally made up the three bottles, I thought there was no way in the world they'd need that much. Then, partway through the night, I was wondering if I'd have enough.

I stumbled out of bed, my feet feeling as heavy as my eyelids. I took the top off the thermos and carefully poured formula into the bottle inside the glove. I filled it to the top and then resealed the thermos. There was still enough for one more meal. Next I screwed the top back on the bottle, locking the milk into the glove.

"Let's go for a walk, girls," I said softly, not wanting to wake anybody up.

I walked to the door and they scrambled and bounced and chased after me, hitting each other and my legs. Opening the door, I held the bottle out in front of me so they'd go outside, then closed the door after all three of us were out.

On the edge of the stairs I flopped down. The instant the glove was within reach the two babies tried to latch onto a finger. Despite the fact that there were two fingers they could suckle, they both fought over the same one. The other, just as good, leaked a little dribble of milk while they continued to ignore it in favour of the one they were both pursuing. The first couple of times they fought like that I thought that maybe one finger was better than the other. Then I saw that it didn't matter; they fought over both. Whichever the first deer had, the second wanted. Vladimir had explained that this was exactly how it would have been if they were feeding from their mother. He thought that was why the glove was better than simply feeding from two separate bottles. This sort of got them going, acting all greedy, and probably made them eat more.

"That's your first course. Now you have to get a little exercise before you get the rest," I said as I pulled the glove away from them.

I got up and walked. The park was completely deserted. I

wondered if even Vladimir would be up yet.

The air was cool and fresh, and I breathed deeply. Considering how many times I'd been woken up in the night, I should have felt more tired. Instead I felt almost bouncy—sort of like the fawns. I figured I'd crash later on today, but right now I still felt as if I was on a high.

Silently passing by the cage of the leopards, I noticed that they were both standing at the mesh, staring out at us. Yesterday they'd been hiding, and I'd only caught a glimpse of tail and a flash of eye. I knew they'd be more active at night, but the sun was well up in the sky. The two leopards moved along the fence, following as I walked. Why were they so friendly or interested in me? Wait a second! It wasn't me they were interested in. They were both staring at the fawns—at my little babies! I wanted to reach down and pick the two of them up, cradle them in my arms, and protect them.

"Bad cats!" I scolded. "*Very* bad cats! Shoo!" I said, gesturing with my hands.

The leopards ignored me.

I looked to the other side. Kushna was sitting up on a rock in the corner of his cage. He was watching the deer, as well.

"Get your own breakfast!" I yelled at him. "Let's go where you have some friends," I said to the little deer, and they followed me.

Actually, they would have followed me if I had walked right into the tiger's pen. I was their mother, and they would trust me to lead them to the right thing. Parenting had both an up and a down side to it.

I walked until we came to the deer pen. There, behind the mesh, were dozens of their relatives. They all seemed too interested in their breakfast, a number of piles of hay, to even notice our arrival. I ducked under the chain and slumped against the fence, sitting on the grass. Immediately the two deer scrambled on top of each other, trying to reach the glove. I lowered it so they could get it, and they immediately jostled for the same finger.

One clasped it tightly, and I squeezed a flow of milk out of the second finger at the other's face. That got the baby's attention, and it grabbed the second finger and began suckling, as well.

Just off to the side was the beginning of a small pen that Vladimir was building to hold the two fawns. He was hoping he'd get enough time to finish it today so they could spend their first night in it. It was to be built so it was right against the mesh of the big pen. He said that way they would be safe from any marauding animals that might come through the park, like coyotes. They would also be safe from being trampled by the other deer or buffalo, yet would be close enough to make them start thinking they were deer.

I turned my attention to the pen. The buffalo were gathered at the far end of the pen, grazing on a patch of grass, while the deer continued to feed off the bales of hay. I don't know what I expected—the deer to all run over to the mesh and try to hug the missing babies—but I was disappointed at the lack of reaction. It was as if we weren't even there. Couldn't they smell them or something?

There was one thing I noticed that was no longer there—the body of their mother. It was gone. There was nothing in that cage that would have eaten it, so Vladimir must have already removed it. I guess a dead animal wasn't what visitors came to see.

"Good morning, big girl Sarah, and babies."

I jumped. "Hello, Vladimir." I was so lost in my thoughts I hadn't seen him coming. "You're up pretty early."

"This not early. Up for hours."

"But it's not even six," I said, glancing at my watch.

"Six late. Up at four. Best time to see animals, see if healthy. And then must start chores."

"You've already been working?" I asked in amazement.

"Already clean deer pen. Put in new food, bales of hay."

"I noticed you removed their mother."

He nodded. "Have to. Not good to leave. Start to rot, spread disease other animals. All taken care of."

"That's good. These fawns had me up most of the night."

"Job of mummy not easy job. Many responsibilities."

"Will they be like that every night?" I asked. I didn't want to sound selfish, but I did need to sleep.

"First night is worst night. Still feed, but Vladimir fix something so they can feed without big girl Sarah getting up always."

"That would be great," I said. "I was wondering, do you think we could name them? The four of us were talking after the lights went out last night, trying to figure out names. We had some ideas."

"Have ideas is good, but baby deer have names already."

"They do?"

"*Da*. Name themselves."

"But I hoped we could maybe—"

"Too late. I tell names. See big one is—"

"Which one is the big one?" I asked.

"Big one is one not small," Vladimir said with a chuckle. "This one," he added, tapping it on the back.

I looked at it, and then the other. I guess it was a little bit bigger.

"Big one is girl deer, so I name after mummy."

"That's nice," I admitted. "What was the mother's name?"

"Not was, *is*. Mummy called big girl Sarah, so deer now called big deer Sarah."

"You named it after me?"

"Only fair. Lose sleep, gain daughter deers."

"And the other one?" I asked.

"Little deer Samantha."

I couldn't help but smile. Underneath that mangy hair, scruffy beard, and mass of muscle there was a gentle man. It would be something to come back here someday, maybe even next summer, and see my babies all grown up and read their names on a plaque...if they were here.

"Vladimir, can I ask you a question?"

"Da," he said, nodding.

"When I got the gloves, I ran into Mr. Armstrong and—"

"Too bad big girl Sarah not in a car."

"What do you mean?" I questioned.

"If you in a car and run into him, that be good, specially if big car—*really* big car."

I started to laugh. Obviously Vladimir didn't like him any more than he liked Vladimir.

"Maybe hit by car would drive sense into thick head," Vladimir continued.

"Well, when I was talking to him, he mentioned something... Maybe he was joking around about going onto the Internet and finding a place that wanted to buy the fawns, but I was wondering—"

"Pig!" Vladimir said angrily, turning and spitting on the ground. "Man is nothing but dirty pig. No, worse than dirty pig. Pigs nice animals, pigs smart animals, pigs not greedy for money!"

"You mean he would sell the babies?" I asked, although from his comments concerning the lion cubs, I thought I knew the answer already.

"Man would sell own mother if enough money."

"He mentioned something about a petting zoo," I said.

"Petting zoo is no zoo. Place where babies poked and picked up and trampled and hurt by people trying to take pictures and feed junk."

"We can't let that happen to Sarah and Samantha," I said, reaching out and protectively placing my arms around them as they continued to nurse.

"We keep deer at least a while, weeks, maybe month. I tell him too small to leave."

"But then when they're bigger he'll sell them?"

"Maybe, maybe no. Either way, Vladimir can't stop. He owner, so do what wants."

"That doesn't seem fair. There must be something we can do."

"Nothing," Vladimir said. "Nothing, but watch animals leave."

"How often has he done this?"

"Many times. Look around. You see many babies in whole park?"

"No, I don't, but I just thought I hadn't noticed, or maybe there weren't any born."

"Animals have babies when animals happy, and Vladimir make sure animals happy!"

"So there were some births other than the lions and deer?" I asked.

"Many, many, babies this spring. Pair of buffalo, little spider monkeys, litter of three leopards, lion cubs, other deer babies, little goats. Vladimir there for all."

"And they're all gone?"

"All gone 'cept lions and new deers. All sold."

Vladimir's tone had gotten huskier, and the look in his eyes was almost scary—no, more than almost. I was afraid, sitting there looking at him, even though I knew he wasn't mad at me. "And that's why you don't like Mr. Armstrong?"

"Don't like for many reasons. Not just selling animals. Old boss sell animals."

"He did?"

"Sometimes sell, sometimes buy, sometimes lend animals to other parks to breed. Sometimes borrow animals for same. But always, always, love animals."

"And Mr. Armstrong doesn't love them," I said, stating the obvious.

"Does not love anything 'cept money. Sees animals as nothing more than money. Sell animal, get money, buy animal, cost money."

"But if he just keeps selling animals, then eventually there won't be any more animals in the park."

Vladimir nodded sadly. "That plan."

"That's a plan?"

"To close park. To have no more animals."

"You think he wants to close the park?"

"Not think. *Know*."

"But if he wants to close the park, why doesn't he just sell off all the animals now?" I asked.

"Wants to. Can't."

"Why can't he?"

"Ah, Vladimir know something big girl Sarah not know. Vladimir know something new boss not know that Vladimir know," he said, pointing a finger at his head.

"What do you know?" I asked, not really expecting him to tell me.

Vladimir looked around, as if he were scanning the area for spies. Nothing was in view but animals, and I figured that even though they were owned by Mr. Armstrong, they weren't planning on telling him anything, even if they could.

"Old boss die and in will leave park to son," Vladimir said.

"Yeah, you told us about that already."

He nodded. "But didn't tell you what old boss tell me about will."

"What did he tell you?"

"He say he know son not like animals much, so he make what he call condition."

"What kind of condition?"

"Condition say that if he want to get park, then must live here for three years and run as zoo, like his daddy run as zoo. And for three years must sleep in park every night."

"You mean he can't even leave for a week to go on a vacation?"

"*Nyet.* Not week. Not day. Must live every night."

"He must feel like he's trapped here," I said.

"*Da,* like animal in cage. In cage with even angrier animal—wife animal."

"You're right. She doesn't seem like she's the sort of person who likes to live in the country."

"Hate living in country. City girl in city clothes. Hate everything about being here. Always in city. You know funny part?"

"What?"

"She allergic to cats. Can't come in park too long or start sneezing. Very funny."

"Is that why she's always in town?"

"*Da.* In town. Shopping. Boss lady love shopping, spreeing."

"So even if he wants he can't leave. He has to stay here."

"Can't sell yet. Can sell in two more years. Old boss think that if son live with animals for three years, then maybe he learn to love animals."

"And that's not working."

Vladimir scowled and spat on the ground. "Did not like before. Now hates. Blames animals for not being able to leave."

"If he did leave, what would happen?"

"Lose everything."

"Who would get it instead?" I asked.

"Land go to government. It become park where kiddies come and wild animals free to live."

"And the animals that are here already?"

"They go to Vladimir," he said quietly.

"That would be wonderful!"

"Not so wonderful. Vladimir not have place to put animals. If park go, then animals must go."

"Well, maybe Mr. Armstrong won't be able to find anybody to buy the place in two years and—"

"Lots want to buy land."

"What do you mean?"

"Land sold to build houses."

"This would become houses?"

"Lots of houses. Many would be on lake. People love water as much as elephant love water. Land worth lots of money."

"Plus the money he could get from selling the animals."

"That just little money."

"It must be more than a little to support all the things his wife buys," I argued.

"Sell babies. Babies worth much money. Big animals worth little money. Give example. Baby tiger worth five thousand dollars. Big grown tiger worth less than five hundred dollars."

"I didn't know that," I said.

"Little tiger good for taking pictures, and petting zoo, and letting people hold and handle. Lots of people want to buy. Big tiger, nobody handle. Needs cage and food, much food, so not many people want, so not worth much money."

"And is it the same with deer?"

"Same with all animals."

"So all those babies they sold got them a lot of money."

"Only thing worth more than baby cats, like lion and tiger, is dead big tiger."

"How can a dead tiger be worth money? It's already dead."

"*Da,* dead, but not gone. Use parts."

"You mean like the skin for a coat?"

"Skin worth money, but not much. Bones, organs inside body worth much money."

"I don't understand."

"Many people think tiger has magic inside. Grind bones and organs to fix disease or make people strong when they eat in medicines."

"You're joking, right?"

"Not joke. That's why tiger endangered animal. Poachers kill and sell body parts."

"That's just awful—killing a beautiful endangered animal for a few dollars."

"Not few dollars, big girl Sarah. Big dollars."

"How much could a dead tiger be worth?"

"Full-grown male tiger like Kushna worth maybe ninety thousand, maybe hundred thousand."

"Dollars?"

"Dollars. American dollars."

"My goodness, that's an incredible amount of—" I stopped and lowered my voice. "Do the Armstrongs know about this?"

"Know, but can do nothing."

"But if they know, why don't they kill Kushna?" I asked, my voice barely a whisper, as if saying it out loud might make it somehow come true.

"Tiger endangered animal. Protected by international law. Cannot kill animal in park. He kill and he go to jail, and if go to jail, he not live at park and lose everything. So Kushna safe."

"But the deer aren't?" I asked.

"Only endangered animals protected. Tiger, leopards."

"The lions?"

He shook his head. "Lions not endangered. Breed like bunnies. Now no more time to talk. Must work."

"I'll go wake up the others, and we'll eat and help," I said.

"Help would help," Vladimir said. "And, big girl Sarah, things I say, just for you to hear. Nobody else, not even brother."

"I won't tell anybody. Promise."

"Good girl. Much work to do. Later take elephant for bath."

Nick would love that. I started to walk away, my babies bumping against my side, and then turned around. "Vladimir, can I ask you one more question?"

He nodded.

"Why do you stay?"

"Need job. Without job I sent back to Russia."

"But you can get a job doing something else."

"Something with animals?"

"I don't know...maybe."

"No read or write English good. Speak bad."

"Your English isn't that bad. I'm sure you could get something."

"Maybe something, but Vladimir not leaving. Staying here. Watch animals. If I leave, what happens to all animals? Who would watch?"

"I guess nobody," I admitted.

"I stay. I care for animals." He paused. "And I watch. Vladimir stay and make sure new boss no leave, even for one night."

I smiled. "Is that why he doesn't like you?"

Vladimir laughed. "No, no, big girl Sarah, boss doesn't not like Vladimir. Boss *hate* Vladimir. Wishes Vladimir would leave. Wishes Vladimir would go far away, back to Russia. Wish Vladimir would disappear from face of earth. But Vladimir stay. That's what old boss would want."

Chapter 10

All I could see was the very tip of an elephant's trunk sticking out of the water. He was beneath the surface, cooling off, using his trunk like a snorkel to breathe without having to surface.

"That was the very, very best thing of my entire life," Nick said as he stood at my side.

"That was pretty good."

"Pretty good? That was way, way more than pretty good. I was there on top of the elephant, not just riding on it like some carnival ride, but steering it, telling it where to go!"

Nick and Vladimir had gotten up onto the back of the elephant in the pen and then ridden him on the trip to the lake. Vladimir had told Nick the four basic elephant commands, and then Nick had been in control, giving orders. Amazingly the elephant listened! If he wasn't my brother, I would have admitted that it really, really was something. I'd even snapped a couple of pictures of him up there without him knowing. I thought I'd blow one up, put it in a frame, and give it to him for a Christmas present. As well, Samantha had been filming a lot of it with her video camera, and I was hoping that somehow I could get a copy of that, too.

"How long do you let him stay in the water?" I asked Vladimir, who was lying on the sand, his eyes closed, hands behind his head.

"He stay as long as like," he said without opening his eyes.

"But shouldn't we be doing something?" I asked.

"Lots of things to do, but they wait," he said, sitting up. "We already work hard."

Vladimir was right. We had worked hard. Before taking the elephant out we'd cut up some more chickens, fed and watered all the animals, and cleaned out two more cages. That was in addition to giving my babies two separate feedings. Those deer could really eat.

"'Sides, big girl Sarah, how you figure we get elephant if he no want to go yet?"

I hadn't really thought about that. It wasn't as if we could go in and get him.

"You bring bathing suit like told?" Vladimir asked.

"Sure, it's under my clothes."

"Good. Go swim. Water warm. Sand soft. Enjoy."

Samantha and Danny were already in the water splashing around.

"Nick, are you coming, too?" I asked.

"Definitely. I figured I'd swim out to Peanuts and see if he wants to play."

I grabbed Nick by the arm. "Is that okay, Vladimir? Is that safe?"

"Not so safe. Peanuts is playful elephant. May grab Nicki and throw him around like water toy."

"Did you hear that?" I asked Nick.

"I heard. I'll stay in the shallows. Can I ride him home again?"

"You ride."

"Excellent," Nick said, and he headed off to the water.

"You go in, too, big girl Sarah."

"Um...I was wondering if I should go back and check the deer."

"Deer fine," Vladimir said. "You feed before come. Fine by selves in little pen till you return."

"I guess you're right."

"Of course right. Vladimir almost always right with animals."

"I was wondering. How much are the two fawns worth?"

"Not sure. Maybe four or five hundred dollars for pair. Why you ask?"

"I was just thinking."

"Thinking if big girl Sarah can buy deer?"

"Well, we do live on a big farm and there'd be plenty of space for them."

"You good mother, but not worry. Maybe deer stay here."

"But you said he's sold all the babies that have been born here."

"*Da,* but all those animals healthy."

I felt my heart skip a beat. "You mean there's something wrong with my deer?"

"Babies healthy."

"That's a relief."

"But only ones who know such thing is Vladimir and big girl Sarah. I tell boss that both very sick, maybe have disease that killed their mummy deer."

"But she didn't die from a disease. It was from giving birth, wasn't it?"

Vladimir smiled. "I know this. You know this. Boss...he know nothing. He believe what I say. I say if he sell sick deer and other animals get sick, then he get in big trouble. Maybe lawyers sue him and he lose much money. He not want to lose much money. He leave deer alone while I keep them in special place away from other animals."

"Like in quarantine?"

"Like in little cage," Vladimir said. "Tell him cannot be with other deer."

"So my deer are safe?" I asked.

"Safe for now. Maybe safe for two years," he said with a shrug. "Who knows."

"I guess nobody."

"All Vladimir know is that bath time over."

"It is?"

"*Da.* Peanuts coming out of water."

I turned and saw the elephant emerge from the lake. In his trunk he was carrying a large log that had been floating in the water. The three kids scrambled along beside him, splashing, jumping, and screaming. Peanuts dropped the log and dipped his trunk back into the water. Then he turned and shot out a spray of water, hitting Nick and nearly knocking him off his feet.

"Peanuts like play," Vladimir said. "Lonely for other elephants since sold. Hard to be by self."

"Is it hard for you?" I asked, blurting out the question without thinking.

Vladimir smiled sadly. "Was easy when old boss round. Now hard. Miss family in Russia. Still, have family here."

"You do? I didn't know that."

He grinned. "Lots family. Peanuts family. Kushna family. Animals like family. And for few days, big girl Sarah, and little girl Samantha, and Nicki, and Danny like family, like little brothers and sisters back home. Come, much work to be done. Kids help with feeding."

"Are they having chicken again for lunch?"

"Special lunch so visitors can see. I call it Feast of the Beasts. Tourists love to see."

After we put Peanuts back in his pen, we all sat together for a quick lunch. Then, while Vladimir was getting the food ready for the big cats, the four of us went back to our cabin and changed out of our bathing suits. Everybody pitched in to give Sarah and Samantha another feeding of formula. I appreciated the help, but I had to admit that I felt a little bit jealous. After all, I was their mother, and it looked as if they were more interested in whoever had the glove than they were in me. It was like my mother always said: "You raise them to leave you."

Suddenly there was a loud rumbling of an engine outside the cabin. For an instant I had the terrible thought that Mr. Armstrong was coming to inspect his property and to see if the

deer really were sick. Then I realized that the sound I was hearing was more like a lawn mower than a fancy car.

"Vladimir's here," Nick said. He was standing at the door.

"Are the babies all put away in their pen?" I asked.

"I put them in myself," Samantha said.

"And the gate's secured so they can't get out?"

"I locked it myself," she said.

"Good. Then we better get going."

Vladimir was sitting on the seat of a little tractor. The engine
was rumbling noisily, and a stream of smelly black smoke came
out of the exhaust. Behind the tractor was a small trailer. It held
three large containers, each overflowing with meat for the big cats.

"Tourists waiting. You four take shortcut through woods. I
drive round and meet by leopard cage."

There was already a large crowd of visitors gathered at the
chain in front of the leopards' pen. The Feast of the Beast was a
big draw at the park. We'd missed it yesterday because we had
to care for the fawns. Even though I'd seen Buddha eat a hundred
times and had been part of feedings here already, I was still
looking forward to it.

We came up to the back of the crowd. Danny, Nick, and
Samantha started to wind their way through the people, trying to
get a spot up by the front. I was too old to do that. Instead I
climbed onto a large rock where I could see over everybody's
heads.

I heard the sound of the tractor and saw it bumping down
the path. Vladimir slowed and brought it to a stop near the edge
of the crowd. He climbed off the tractor and went to the trailer.
Hoisting one of the containers of meat, he put it on his shoulder
and started moving through the crowd toward the pen. As he
stepped over the chain, the leopards came bounding toward the
fence. They snarled and snapped and fought each other, scrambling to get right up to the section of the mesh directly in front of
where Vladimir stood. He put the container on the ground and

turned to face the crowd.

"Good afternoon. My name is Vladimir. I head trainer and zookeeper at Exotic Animal World. I feed cats starting with leopard. While feed animals I talk about animals. If you have question, I try to answer. So I start."

Vladimir bent down and grabbed two slabs of meat from the container. They were red and raw and cut into long, thin pieces. There were bones—maybe rib bones—protruding from them. "These are leopards. From Africa. Live in many parts, jungle, forest, and plain. Many parts.

Inside the cage one of the cats was standing on its hind legs, tail twitching, watching Vladimir's every move. The second cat, a smaller female, was a dozen feet away, crouched, its tail moving back and forth. Vladimir took one of the slabs of meat and pushed it through a porthole in the fence. The cat greedily grabbed the meat from his hands. Quickly Vladimir took the second piece of meat, reached in through the hole, and pitched it in the direction of the second cat. She jumped up and grabbed it in midair.

"Leopards small big cat. Big for animal, but small compared to cat like tiger or lion," he said as he reached down and grabbed two more pieces of meat. When he pushed them through the hole, the male leopard grabbed them both in his mouth and dropped them in a corral formed by his paws. The cat was guarding them, stopping his mate from getting near his food.

"Typical male. Doesn't want to share," a woman joked.

"Typical all animals," Vladimir said. "Big animals no want share with little animals."

"All animals?" the same woman asked.

"All cats. Even cats that hunt as pack like lions. Big eat first, then little animals get leftover scraps. Here Vladimir feed, so all animals get food." Vladimir reached back into the food container and grabbed more meat. Two pieces were tossed to the little female, and another slab was dropped at the feet of the big cat.

"Leopard is good hunter, good killer of animals. Many times

it kill, and then lions come and chase leopard away. Leopard is only small big cat," he said. "So for safety, it take animal in mouth, jump into tree, and climb high."

"Why don't the lions just climb up after him?" a man asked. He was wearing funny-looking shorts and a shirt to match and had three cameras draped around his neck.

"Lions no climb trees."

"Couldn't they just jump?" the man asked.

"Not jump high enough. Leopard jump high and then climb to safe place."

"And it jumps carrying the animal it killed?" the same man asked.

"*Da.* Can jump eight feet up tree with antelope in mouth."

"No way," the man said, shaking his head. "I think you're wrong."

"Wrong? You think Vladimir wrong?" he asked, waving a piece of meat and taking a step toward the guy in a threatening manner.

"He's right!" I said, and the entire crowd turned to face me.

"Leopards can do that. I've seen it—when I was on safari in Africa."

"You were on safari?" Samantha asked.

"Tell them all about it," Nick said. "Go ahead," he taunted.

"Um...when I was in Africa on safari...from the jeep I saw the leopards."

"Who is this girl?" the man asked.

"World expert here to visit today," Vladimir said. "Expert."

"She's just a girl," somebody else said.

"Not girl. Twenty-seven year-old woman."

Twenty-seven! I was lucky if I could pass for sixteen!

"And as special treat...Dr. Sarah will help me today in tour."

I looked down at Nick, standing in the crowd, smirking. He was enjoying this.

"I'd be glad to," I said. Maybe I wasn't twenty-seven, and maybe

I wasn't a world-famous expert, but I did know a thing or two about animals, at least more than anybody standing in the crowd.

❧

"You two are really starting to annoy me," I said to the little deer as they bounded and pranced around. And I thought having a little brother was bad enough.

"Can't you make them stop?" Nick asked, his voice coming out of the darkness over my head from his bunk.

"Yeah, we need to get some sleep," Samantha added from across the room.

"I can't help it. They're just being playful. They'll settle down," I pleaded.

"You said that half an hour ago," she said.

"And when you brought them in," Nick added. "Vladimir said they don't even need to be here, that they can sleep in that pen."

"By themselves at night in the dark?"

"It's always dark at night, Sarah," Nick said. "And they don't have to be alone in their pen."

"They don't?"

"No, you can sleep there, too, if you want," Nick said.

"Thanks a lot."

"Come on, Sarah. Vladimir said it would be okay, so it'll be okay. Please," Nick begged. "We need to get some sleep."

"I don't know."

"Come on, Sarah, it might even be better for them to be in the pen," Nick added.

"How do you figure that?"

"Because then they can get to know the other deer, and the other deer can get to know them."

He had a point. Vladimir had completed the small pen attached to the side of the big deer pen. That way they were right there with their extended family but were still safely in their own pen where nobody could accidentally step on them.

One of the deer bounced up onto her hind legs and butted me in the side. Maybe it wouldn't be such a bad idea for them to be in there tonight. They'd just been fed, and I'd feed them again first thing in the morning. Besides, it wasn't just the other three kids who were being cheated out of their sleep. I needed sleep just as much, if not more.

"Okay, I'll put them in their pen."

"Great!" Samantha said.

"Fantastic!" Danny seconded.

"Finally," Nick said with a sigh.

"So who's going to go with me?" I asked.

Suddenly the room was quiet. The only sound was the clip-clopping of little deer hooves on the wooden floor.

"Somebody should help me," I said.

"Why?" Nick asked. "None of us wanted them here tonight except you. Besides, it isn't as if they're going to wander away from you. Wherever you go they'll follow."

"I just don't think I should have to go by myself."

"It's not far, Sarah. You could be there and back in the time it's taking you to argue about it. Just go."

I wanted to argue, and I still didn't think it was fair, but I knew it would be faster to just do it myself. When I climbed out of bed, the two fawns got even friskier, jumping up at me. They must have figured it was feeding time again. As they tried to latch onto my fingers, they seemed more like baby pigs than baby deer. They'd come to associate fingers with the glove, and the glove with food, so they were always trying to suckle my fingers. I pulled my hands up, reached over, and flicked the light switch, bathing the room in bright light.

"What's the idea!" Nick screamed.

"Hey!" Danny yelled.

I smiled. "I'm so sorry. I couldn't find my shoes without turning on the light."

I turned it off again. I knew exactly where my shoes were located. I just thought I shouldn't be the only one who had to get more awake.

With the deer at my feet, I started out the door. Besides slipping on my sneakers, I'd also taken a little flashlight from the top of the dresser. Stepping outside, I flicked it on. A small beam of light shone a dozen feet ahead of me, illuminating the path.

Up above it seemed like a million stars twinkled at me. It was hard to believe, but these were the same stars that sparkled above my house right now—the same stars that were in the sky above my mother's head somewhere in the Caribbean. It was amazing how bright it was.

I turned the flashlight off. It took a few seconds for my eyes to adjust, and then I could see even better than before. Now my sight wasn't limited to just the beam of light. I could also see into the dimly lit distance.

The gravel crunched under my feet as I walked. I listened for other sounds. I knew this was the most active time for some of the animals in the park. With their keen ears, better vision, and sense of smell, they were all observing me in one way or another as I moved along. That was a strange thought. All along the path, on both sides, behind the fencing, were some of the most dangerous and fierce animals in the entire world. Yet we were safe as long as we were on the path. But what about other animals? Things like wolves, coyotes, and bears naturally lived in this area. Vladimir had said they put away the donkeys, goats, chickens, and ducks every night so nothing could get them. Suddenly I didn't feel so safe. Maybe I should have brought a big stick instead of a little flashlight. This didn't seem like such a short trip. I wanted to do two very different things now: I wanted to move faster and more quietly.

"Come on, girls," I whispered.

We rounded Kushna's pen, and I looked over and was captured by two sharp points of yellow light—his eyes. I froze, then focused my eyes until I could vaguely see the outline of his body. He was right by the fence, crouched and watching us. I felt a chill rise out of my feet and go all the way up my legs and into my spine. My brain told me he was behind the fence and I was safe. My heart and gut weren't so sure. I needed to get away. I turned, then was startled by a sound. Voices.

I looked up. Coming along the path was a beam of light—no, two separate beams of light. It couldn't be Vladimir, at least not by himself. Maybe it was Mr. Armstrong. And here I was with the two fawns. He hadn't seen them yet, and I was hoping we could keep it that way. Even to somebody who knew nothing about animals it would be pretty obvious there was nothing wrong with either of these two.

Just off to the side was a small wooden structure. It had a roof and half walls, and Vladimir had said it had been used as a snack bar before they put in all the vending machines. I ducked and moved toward it, the deer by my side. When I pushed open the gate, it creaked a bit, causing me to shudder. They were still too far down the path to hear the noise. I figured I'd stay in here with the babies until they passed. Maybe he was headed for the temporary pen to look at the deer. It would be good if he went there and didn't see them, because we could say they were still too sick to be outside.

The voices got louder, and I poked my head over the wall to watch. It was impossible to see anybody coming up behind the lights, but I did recognize one of the voices as Mr. Armstrong's. The second, also male, was definitely not Vladimir. What were they doing out here, and who was the person with Mr. Armstrong?

I became aware that each deer had latched on to a different hand, so I had one deer suckling from my left hand, and the other from my right. That was more than okay. This way they'd be quiet for the thirty seconds we'd need for the men to pass by.

The lights came closer and closer. I ducked, held my breath, and waited.

"This is the pen," I heard Mr. Armstrong say.

Great—they were standing just outside my hiding spot!

"We may not see him right away, because it's a big space and—there he is!" Mr. Armstrong cried. "It's almost as if he were waiting for us to come!"

"How old is he?" the man asked.

"Almost twelve," Mr. Armstrong said.

I knew that was a lie. Kushna was closer to twenty.

"And his weight?"

"Over eight hundred pounds."

"Excellent. The bigger the better," the man said.

"We feed him well. A healthy tiger is a happy tiger."

"I didn't think you cared much about whether they were happy or not," the man said.

I was shocked by his statement. Whoever this guy was, he not only knew what Mr. Armstrong was like, but he wasn't afraid to say it.

"And you're prepared to part with him? Is that correct?"

"If the price is right," Mr. Armstrong said.

That explained why he was here looking at the animals. The only interest he had in them was for what they were worth.

"I think we can make it worth your while," the man said. "I was thinking forty."

Forty dollars! He couldn't sell him for that little. Vladimir said a grown tiger was worth more like five hundred dollars. Was Mr. Armstrong stupid?

"You'd better think again. I know he's worth more."

At least he wasn't completely stupid.

"I was thinking more like ninety," Mr. Armstrong said.

Wrong again. He was stupid.

The man chuckled. "Then perhaps we had better come to some middle ground."

"I'm listening," Mr. Armstrong said.

And so was I. I peeked over the wall and was shocked to see they were no more than a dozen feet from me. Directly in front of them sat Kushna. Crouching down, he stared past the two men to where the deer and I were hiding. He couldn't see us, but he certainly could smell our scent.

"You have obviously read or heard about the prices for a tiger," the man said.

"I know the going price is much closer to my figure than it is to yours."

"But you're asking me to take all the risks. I must transport and distribute the tiger, while you do nothing more than sign a paper and take the money. If something happens, you can just sit back and claim you didn't know anything. Who knows? You might even turn on me, hanging me out to dry if things go wrong."

"I wouldn't do that," Mr. Armstrong protested.

The man snorted. "There is little honor among thieves. You give less, you get less money."

"How much less?" Mr. Armstrong asked. He didn't sound very confident

"The figure is forty-three."

"Then we can't do business!"

"Perhaps we can't," the man said. He seemed calm, cool, and collected—as if he knew he held all the cards. "Take me back to my car and let's not waste any more time."

"Wait!"

"For what?"

"I want to do business, honestly!" Mr. Armstrong said. "I just need a higher figure."

This was ridiculous! I'd give him a hundred dollars if he'd leave Kushna alone and—"*ommmppp!*" I yelped, stifling the sound caused by one of the deer biting hard on one of my fingers.

"What was that?" the man asked.

"Could have been anything. We're surrounded by animals."

"And nobody else is here?"

"The park has been closed for five hours. We're alone."

There was a long and painful silence. What were they waiting for?

"Now what were you saying?" the man asked.

"I told you I need more money."

"If you want a higher figure, you must be prepared to take more risk."

"What do you mean?" Mr. Armstrong asked, and I wondered the same thing.

"You must be there while we transport the tiger."

"I can do that."

"And you must be there when the procedure is done," the man added.

Procedure—what procedure? What was he talking about?

"I...I guess I could do that."

"And I want you to put it all in writing."

"You're asking me to put my neck in a noose," Mr. Armstrong complained.

"No, I'm asking you to do something to earn the money I am going to pay you."

"And how much is that?"

"Sixty-five. Think about how many pairs of shoes that could buy your wife."

I'd seen her shoes. Sixty-five dollars wouldn't buy one shoe, let alone a pair.

"I don't like it," Mr. Armstrong said.

Good. Maybe he'd come to his senses.

"But I'll do it," he continued.

"Excellent!" the man said. "I'll be here the day after tomorrow. I suggest we make the move at this time of night or later."

"Fine," Mr. Armstrong said. "And you'll have the money with you?"

"Cash. Small bills. Sixty-five thousand dollars."

Thousand! Sixty-five thousand dollars! There was no way a tiger was worth that much money...unless it was a dead tiger.

Chapter 11

I knocked on Vladimir's door. I wanted to pound on it, yell for him to answer, but I couldn't. Sound travelled far in the night air, and while I wanted Vladimir to hear me, I didn't want the Armstrongs or that man to notice me.

"Vladimir!" I called softly, pressing my face against his door. "Come on, Vladimir, open up, please, it's important." I was pretty sure I'd be waking him up and getting him out of bed—anybody who was up at four in the morning was definitely in bed long before eleven at night.

I knocked again, this time as loud as I dared. I heard something, somebody, moving inside!

"Leave me alone!" Vladimir's voice boomed through the door. He sounded angry. The door flew open. "I sleeping so just leave alone—" He stopped mid-sentence, his eyes opening wide.

I took a deep breath. He was wearing a long, wide night-gown that looked almost like a dress, and on his head was a long cap. He looked like somebody from an old-time movie, or even a fairy tale.

"Big girl Sarah, it is you!"

"Who were you expecting?"

He snarled. "Expecting to be bothered by boss man or wife. Always bothering Vladimir. Why you here?"

"I needed to talk to you."

"In middle of night?"

"It's not the middle of the night. It's only eleven-thirty."

"That middle of night for me. Can wait till morning?"

"No, I need to talk to you right now. It's important! Mr. Armstrong is going to sell Kushna."

"Kushna? No, no, must be wrong. No one want to buy old mangy tiger."

"Yes, they do—for a lot of money."

"No, must be wrong. Kushna too old to be wanted even for little money."

"They're going to kill him!" I exclaimed.

Vladimir's mouth dropped open, and the colour drained from his face.

"And Mr. Armstrong is going to be there, and they're talking about money, a whole lot of money and—"

"Wait, wait!" Vladimir said. "Come, come into house. Sit down, calm down, talk," he said as he ushered me in.

I came in and sat at the kitchen table.

"Big girl Sarah, you want drink?"

"I'm okay, well, sure, I guess...thanks." After Mr. Armstrong and the man left, I'd rushed to put the deer away in their little pen and then run all the way here without stopping.

"Vladimir need drink," he said, walking over to the fridge and opening it. He grabbed a pitcher of orange juice and two glasses from the cupboard, then filled one glass to the top and handed it to me. The second he only filled halfway.

"Need extra special thing in Vladimir's drink," he explained, opening a cupboard above the fridge and pulling out a bottle of vodka. Unscrewing the cap, he poured the clear liquid into his glass until it was as full as mine.

"*Vashe Zdorovye!*" Vladimir said as he raised his glass and clinked it against mine. Then he raised his glass to his lips and drained it in one gulp, wiping his mouth with the back of his hand.

I took a sip from my glass.

"Now tell me things," Vladimir said. "How you hear? What you hear?"

"I heard Mr. Armstrong talking to a man."

"Little man?" Vladimir asked.

"I couldn't really tell. I think he was smaller than Mr. Armstrong. Do you know who he is?"

"Have idea. Animal business has bad men. Always trying to get animals. Tried to buy from old boss. We know what he really wanted, so not sell to him. Did he have beady little eyes and face like weasel?"

"It was too dark to see his face, especially from where I was hiding."

"You hiding?"

I explained to him where I was when I overheard them talking.

"And you hear them making deal for tiger?"

"I heard. They were talking about a lot of money. Sixty-five thousand dollars."

"That is blood money. Money to slaughter Kushna. You hear when this happen?"

"The day after tomorrow, late at night. That doesn't leave us much time."

"No need much time. Only need one minute," he said as he got up from the table.

"One minute to do what?" I asked anxiously.

"One minute to go up to boss house."

"Do you think talking to him will help?" I asked.

"No," Vladimir said, shaking his head. "Talking not help, but Vladimir not go to talk."

"What are you going to do?"

"Going to break arms of boss," he said as he turned and left the room.

"You can't do that!" I yelled, jumping up from the table and starting after him.

"Sure can break arm. He not big like Vladimir. Could break arms and legs and neck of boss...easy."

"That isn't what I mean. If you do that, you'll be arrested!"

Vladimir stopped and turned to face me. He nodded. "Big girl Sarah, right, not break arms."

Thank goodness he realized that—

"Instead of breaking arms, just threaten to break arms!"

"You can't do that, either!" I protested. "It's just as illegal to threaten somebody as it is to actually do it. You'll be arrested just the same if he calls the police." I paused. "But maybe we should call the police."

"Police no good. Boss just say he selling tiger. Not wrong to sell tiger."

"But it is illegal to kill one, isn't it?"

"Is against law. If can prove. Can big girl Sarah prove he want to slaughter?"

"Well, I heard them talking about it. Maybe the police will believe me."

"Even if believe, probably not do anything."

"Why wouldn't they?" I asked.

"Local police, local laws. Killing tiger is *international* law."

"Isn't there sort of like an international police department?" I asked. "You know, somebody to enforce international laws."

Vladimir shrugged and shook his head.

"I know who would know."

"Who?" he asked.

"Mr. McCurdy. He knows everything about tigers. I just wish he was here so I could ask him."

"Call on phone," Vladimir suggested.

"He doesn't have a phone, but I do know how to get hold of him. I can call my friend Erin. She'll go out and get him and he can call us here at your place."

"Vladimir not have phone."

"But Samantha does!" I exclaimed, remembering the cell

phone she had at the airport.

"We go and talk on phone," Vladimir said, jumping to his feet and starting for the door. Then he stopped. "Better still, big girl Sarah make call. Vladimir change into clothes."

❧

"My mother said I could only use the phone for an emergency," Samantha said.

"This is an emergency!" I practically yelled.

"It better be an emergency after you made us all get up," Nick said.

"It is. Let me use the phone and I'll explain it."

Reluctantly Samantha handed me the phone. I looked at it tentatively. "How do you turn it on?"

"The button on the very bottom," she said.

I pushed it and the phone beeped and flashed, then lights came on, illuminating the number pad. I started to dial Erin's number.

"I hope the person you're calling thinks this is as important as you do," Nick said.

"What do you mean?" I asked as the first ring sounded in my ear.

"Because our mom would go ballistic if anybody called *us* this late."

"Oh, my goodness, I hadn't thought about—"

"Hello," answered a very sleepy male voice—Erin's father.

"Um, hello, I'm really, really sorry to call you this late, but I really need to talk to Erin. It's an emergency."

"Who's this?" he asked.

"It's Sarah. Sarah Fraser."

"Sarah? Aren't you away on holidays?"

"Yeah, me and my brother."

"And are you okay? Is your brother okay? Is everything all

right?" he asked, sounding alarmed.

"We're okay. It's just that there's an emergency and we have to get a message through to Mr. McCurdy."

"What sort of an emergency?"

"There's a tiger, and if we can't get a hold of Mr. McCurdy, it's going to die."

"Sounds serious. I'll go and wake up Erin."

"Thank you so much."

I heard the receiver being put down and voices in the background.

"Kushna's sick?" Nick asked.

"He's close to being dead," I said.

"Can't Vladimir help him, or can't they call in a vet?" Samantha questioned.

"It's not something Vladimir can—"

"Hello, Sarah!" Erin said through the phone.

"Erin, thank God! I need you to get to Mr. McCurdy and tell him I need his help. Please. I'll give you a phone number where he can reach me. It's really important."

"I'll go right now," she said. "At least if..."

I couldn't hear and I certainly couldn't see what was happening at the other end, but I could picture Erin looking at her father, pleading with her eyes.

"Dad?" she asked. There was a pause. "Oh, thank you so much!" she almost screamed. "We can go out tonight. Now give me the phone number where you can be reached. "

"Thank you so much Erin, and please thank your father."

"It's not a problem. That's what friends are for, and that's what friends' fathers are for. He'll get the message within an hour."

"Great. Thank you, and good night."

I jumped up and practically landed on my feet. I hadn't realized I'd fallen asleep. It was bright and sunny—it must be morning. I was still clutching the cell phone in my hand; Mr. McCurdy hadn't phoned. Danny was curled in a little ball at the end of Samantha's bed, sound asleep. Samantha was part on, part off her bed, her eyes closed, also asleep. On the upper bunk Nick was asleep, a pillow clutched tightly in both hands and pulled over his face. He had never looked lovelier.

"Wake up, Nick," I said, grabbing the pillow away from him and tossing it across the room. "Get up!" I yelled. "All of you wake up!"

Everybody quickly climbed out of bed without complaining.

"Where's Vladimir?" Nick asked.

"I don't know. He wasn't here when I woke up."

"Did Mr. McCurdy phone?" he asked.

"No, he didn't," I said quietly. That worried me. It wasn't like him not to follow through with something, and he'd promised he'd help if we called. Maybe Erin didn't get him.

"Maybe the cell phone isn't working," Nick suggested.

"It's working," Samantha protested. "It's a good phone. Let me see it," she said, taking it from me.

"No wonder you couldn't get a call," she said. "It's turned off."

"I didn't turn it off," I said. "Honestly."

"Maybe you rolled on it in your sleep and hit the off button," Danny suggested.

Samantha pushed a button, the phone beeped, and then came to life, lighting up. Then it shut down again.

"It's out of power," Samantha said. "That's why it wasn't on—it turned itself off."

"Great, just great," I sighed.

"I can recharge it," Samantha offered. "I can do it right now."

"How long will it take?" Nick asked.

"A few hours—six or seven, I think. My mother always plugs it in at night, and it's charged when we wake up in the morning."

"That's too long," Nick said. "We need to talk to Mr. McCurdy before that. Maybe Vladimir can drive us into town."

"He can't," I said. "The van still isn't working."

"Maybe we can walk," Danny said.

"It's about a two-hour walk," Samantha said. "Each way. That's a long way to walk."

"Besides, we have things to do here," I said. "Regular chores, feeding the fawns, and then we have to watch Kushna. Somebody always has to watch him."

"I thought they weren't coming until tomorrow night," Nick said.

"Vladimir said you can't predict what these people will do. Maybe the guy will come back today to have a look at Kushna, and we can see what he looks like. You can't tell with these people."

"I still don't get it," Danny said.

"Get what?" I asked.

"Why a tiger would be worth that much money. Do they eat it or something?"

"Sort of, but not really," I answered. "I'll try to explain. Lots of people think tigers are very special animals."

"They are special animals," Danny said.

"Of course they are. But they think they have magical powers, and the way people get those powers is to use parts of the animal."

"What do you mean 'use'?" Danny asked.

"They take things like the organs—the heart, liver, and gall bladder—as well as the bones, and they include them in pills and ointments."

"Like medicines?"

"The people who make them and use them think they're medicines, but they're not. There's no scientific proof that they help anybody or anything. The only thing that's for sure is that tigers are killed to make these potions. Slaughtered by stupid people."

"Nobody's going to do that to Kushna," Danny said.

"Not if we can help it," I said. "I just wish I could have spoken to Mr. McCurdy. He'd know what to do. I know he would."

"Then we don't have any choice," Nick said. "I'm going to walk to town to call Mr. McCurdy."

"You can't go by yourself," I said.

"Then I'll go with him," Danny volunteered.

"That's no better. You're too little."

"How about if I went with him?" Samantha asked. "We could take care of each other, and then Danny could stay here with you to help out with the animals."

"I don't know," I said.

"What else can we do?" Nick asked.

"I don't know."

"Well, it's like mom always says, sometimes you don't have any good choices, so you have to choose the one that's the least bad," Nick said. "And this is the best I can think of."

"Well?" Samantha prodded.

"Okay," I reluctantly agreed.

"Great," she said. "We'll get dressed, eat, and go right away. If we move fast, we can be back by noon."

"Just be careful," I said to Nick. "And I want you to go out through the back gate."

"Why?" Nick asked.

"I don't want to risk you being seen by the Armstrongs," I explained.

"Yes...big girl Sarah," Nick said, imitating Vladimir.

Samantha chuckled.

"Both of you."

She smiled. She wasn't a bad kid...but she still *was* kind of bossy.

❧

Vladimir rumbled off on the tractor, pulling the meat wagon, and the crowd disappeared along with him, scrambling to get a good viewing spot at the next cage. Danny was sitting on the back of the tractor, and waved to me as they left. I waved back. I waited for the last straggler to pass and then moved in the opposite direction. I ducked under the chain that surrounded Kushna's pen. He was sitting very close to the fence, a pile of ribs in front of him. He was chewing on a piece of meat, and I could hear his teeth crunching the bones.

He was the same type of tiger as Mr. McCurdy's cat, Buddha. They were both Siberian tigers, the biggest of the big cats, weighing up to eight hundred pounds. While I couldn't be completely sure without having them side by side, I thought Kushna was bigger. What I was sure about was the difference in their age and appearance. Buddha was only about five years old and looked, well, younger—more fit. It wasn't that Kushna had grey fur or a cane or a little walker, but he was obviously older. It was the same way you could tell with a dog. When they were young, they were frisky and playful, and there was a look in their eyes. Maybe that didn't sound very scientific, but I knew I was right.

Kushna got up, stretched, and came in my direction. I stopped breathing and took a half step away from the mesh. I knew in my head he couldn't get me, but still, there was something about seeing a tiger coming toward you—something that caused a chill to go up your spine, that caused you to want to run or hide or climb a tree. Maybe it was a small leftover part of the human brain that had been there since we weren't much more than a fancy monkey sitting in a tree, something that said be afraid...be very afraid.

Kushna still had a piece of meat sticking out the side of his mouth. He came over and dropped it right at his feet—at *my* feet.

"Is that for me, boy?" I asked.

In answer, he pressed his head against the mesh and

rubbed, pushing it back. I looked at the mesh. It was tight and small and he couldn't get a paw through. He rubbed again, and this time rose slightly on his hind legs. I put a hand against the fence, careful to keep my fingers on my side, and pressed back. I could feel his fur and muscle against me.

"You're a good boy, aren't you, Kushna?" I said.

He rubbed again.

"I have a friend who'd love to meet you. His name is Buddha. You two could be buddies."

Kushna turned his head to the side and looked at me with those gigantic yellow eyes. He looked thoughtful, as if he understood what I was saying.

"It must be hard to be here by yourself without any other tigers. I wouldn't like it at all. It must be hard...for both you and Buddha. It would be something to get the two of you together."

Kushna flicked out his tongue, and the tip went through the mesh and met my hand. I didn't draw away. He was just giving me a little kiss. It made no sense, but I couldn't help but think that somehow Kushna knew we were trying to help, that he knew he was in danger and that we were there to protect him. If only Mr. McCurdy were here. I looked at my watch. It was almost two o'clock. Nick and Samantha were supposed to be back by noon. At least that was the time we figured it would take them. I was getting more worried by the minute. It was bad enough wondering if they were able to speak to Mr. McCurdy without wondering where they were and if anything bad had happened to them.

I tried to reason with myself. Our farm was about the same distance from the closest town as this park was to the place they were headed. Nick had walked that dozens of times. He was okay. They were both okay. I just hadn't estimated the time right. Maybe it was farther than I thought, or maybe they couldn't find a pay phone right away, or maybe Erin wasn't in and they were waiting until they could speak to her, or maybe they spoke to her and they were waiting for a call back from Mr. McCurdy...or maybe they were dead, lying on the side of the road after being hit by a passing transport truck whose driver was drunk and—

"Don't be stupid!" I said to myself.

"Pardon me?"

I turned around. There was an older woman pushing a baby stroller.

"I was talking to myself," I said, feeling embarrassed.

"Oh...should you be in there?" she asked. "I think we're supposed to remain behind the chains."

"It's okay. I'm staff. I work here."

"Oh, that's nice. So you get to play with the animals."

"I get to be around them."

"That tiger seems to really like you," the woman said.

I looked at Kushna. He seemed to be smiling at me. "Yes, he does. And I like him, too."

"It isn't as if we could call you or anything," Nick said.

"And we rushed back as quickly as we could," Samantha added.

"You had me worried."

"You're always worried," Nick replied.

"That's because you always give me something to worry about."

"And now you're worried about Mr. McCurdy," Nick said.

"Not worried. Just concerned."

"Too bad the whole thing—the walk to town, waiting, all the phone calls—were for nothing," Samantha said.

"Yeah, what a waste," Nick said. "I wish we could have at least gotten hold of Erin. We called a dozen times, and all we could get was the answering machine."

"I wish you could have talked to her, too," I said. "Then we would have known for sure that she's talked to Mr. McCurdy."

"I'm sure she talked to him," Nick said. "She promised to do it right away. Right?"

"You're right," I said. "Of course she went out. I just want to know what Mr. McCurdy said. I wish we could hear from him. Your phone should be recharged by now, shouldn't it?"

"For sure. I'll go and get it right now," Samantha said.

"I'll come with you," Danny offered, and the two of them went off.

"Maybe I should go, too," Nick offered.

"I've got a better idea. How about if you stay here and watch Kushna?"

"And what are you going to do?"

I looked at my watch. It was almost four o'clock. "It's time for me to feed the girls. I'll give them a good feeding, grab a snack, and I'll come right back and take over watching Kushna. It's better that I'm here, anyway, because I'm the only one who could recognize that guy who was with Mr. Armstrong."

"Do you really think we need to watch the tiger during the day?" Nick asked. "Couldn't I help you with the feeding?"

"I don't know."

"It isn't as if he's going to try to take him during the day."

"I guess you're right." I paused. "But once the park is closed for the day somebody's going to have to be here at all times right through the night."

"That could be kind of cool."

"I don't know about cool, but it certainly will be cold," I said.

"We better dress warm and bring along some blankets."

"That's not what I want to have with me tonight."

"What do you want to have?" Nick asked.

"Mr. McCurdy," I said.

"Did somebody say my name?"

Chapter 12

"Mr. McCurdy!" I gasped.

"Good to see you haven't forgotten me."

I rushed over and threw my arms around him. He staggered slightly, and for a split second I thought the two of us were going to topple over.

"Careful, Sarah, at my age if I break I don't heal too fast."

"You're here...you're here," I sighed with relief.

"Course I'm here."

"But how?" Nick asked.

Mr. McCurdy reached over and threw an arm around Nick's shoulder. "Drove."

"But it's over eight hundred kilometres."

"Eight hundred and twenty-seven, maybe a few less. I made a wrong turn outside town. You two look shocked to see me."

"We are."

"I don't know why. You called Erin and said it was an emergency."

"I just thought you'd call," I said.

"I did for almost two hours. Couldn't get through."

"The phone died," I said sheepishly.

"Erin told me it was life and death, that you had a sick tiger, and I know that the first few hours are the most dangerous, so I had no time to lose. I threw my medicine bag in the car, and me and Calvin jumped in and—"

"Calvin's here?" Nick asked in disbelief.

"He's sleeping in the car. Poor ape loves car rides, but he's too old to stay up that long."

"How long have you been up?" I asked. He looked tired, his hair flying in a hundred different directions and a layer of grey stubble on his face.

"Erin woke me up around two in the morning, and I started to drive, and it's now—"

"After four in the afternoon," I said. "I can't believe you drove all the way here."

Mr. McCurdy shrugged. "I heard there was a sick tiger. 'Sides, I promised you two that if there was anything you needed I'd be there for you, so here I am."

"You're...you're...the best," I stammered.

Mr. McCurdy looked embarrassed. "I've been called a lot of things in my day—most of which I couldn't repeat in front of a fine young lady like yourself—but this is the first time I been called that."

"She's right, Mr. McCurdy," Nick said, and Mr. McCurdy gave a sly little smile in response.

"You must be as tired as Calvin," I said. "Do you want to sit down or rest?"

"There'll be time to rest later. I need to see that tiger right away."

Nick and I exchanged a look. What was he going to think when he found out the tiger wasn't sick?

"I'm just surprised that Russell would need my help," Mr. McCurdy said.

"Russell? Who's Russell?" I asked.

"Russell Armstrong. I recognized the place when I drove up. Is he still the owner?"

"Yes, I mean, no. He did own it, but he died."

"Awful sad, but I guess that's no surprise. He would have been close to eighty by now."

"I'm surprised you knew Mr. Armstrong," I said.

"The exotic animal world ain't that big. Eventually everybody gets to know everybody. Not that I knew him well, but we had our dealings. He was a crusty old man, but he knew animals and cared about them."

"That's what Vladimir said," I said.

"Who's Vladimir?"

"He's like the head animal guy," I explained. "He knows lots of things about animals, not like you or Mr. Armstrong, but he's smart."

"Maybe you better bring me to him, and we can start talking about what's ailing his tiger."

"Definitely I want you to meet him, but I can tell you what's wrong," I said.

"Good. What's the problem?" Mr. McCurdy asked.

"The problem is that he's got less than a day and a half until he's dead," Nick said.

"That's not like you to be thinking the worst, Nicholas Fraser. You just have a little faith in me and my medicine bag," Mr. McCurdy said, patting the side of his bag.

"It's not that," I said. "Please let me explain," I said.

"Maybe I'm more tired than I thought, 'cause you ain't making any sense at all, neither of you."

I took a deep breath. "It's like this. The tiger is fine."

"It's fine!" he bellowed. "I drove eight hundred kilometres right through the night, and he's fine?"

"Please keep your voice down," I said, trying to shush him.

"Don't you be shushing me, girl. You may be like a granddaughter to me but—"

"I'm like a granddaughter to you?" I asked, cutting him off.

"Well, I never had one, so I don't know for sure, but if I did—don't go changing the subject! What do you mean the tiger isn't sick? What sort of an emergency is it?"

"He's fine, he's healthy, but what Nick said is true. By this time less than two days from now, if we can't help, the tiger will be dead."

"You're talking nonsense," he said. "Why would anybody want to kill a perfectly healthy— They're going to slaughter it for body parts, aren't they?"

"Yes," I said. "I heard them talking. Please, let's go find Vladimir so we can talk about things and—"

"Hold your horses, girl. This Vladimir fella, is he part of killing this tiger?"

"Never!" I said, shaking my head vigorously. "He's on our side, on the tiger's side. It's all the work of Mr. Armstrong."

"I thought you said he was dead."

"He is. It's his son who owns the place now, but he doesn't care about the animals. He's selling them off, just waiting until he can sell the whole place to build houses and—" I stopped myself as I looked around and realized this whole conversation was taking place with visitors to the park walking all around us. Besides, I was supposed to keep this stuff in the will a secret. I'd promised Vladimir, but maybe he could tell Mr. McCurdy, or give me permission to tell.

"How about you come back to our cabin, and Nick will go and get Vladimir?"

"That might be an idea. My legs are starting to feel a tiny bit tired, and I could use something to drink. A good strong cup of java would be just what the doctor ordered."

"Great. Is Calvin okay in the car for now?" I asked.

"He could use something to drink, as well, I figure."

"Okay. Nick, after you find Vladimir, could you go and get Calvin?"

"Sure, it'll be good to see the old ape."

"And bring him in through the back gate."

Nick gave me a questioning look.

"I don't want the Armstrongs to know anything. I think it's better if we don't draw any attention to Mr. McCurdy being here."

"Too late for that," Mr. McCurdy said.

"What do you mean?"

"I was talking to some girl at the front. I tried to explain I was here to help with the tiger, but she didn't seem to understand. Made me pay seven dollars and fifty cents to come through the gate."

"What did she look like?" I asked.

"Young. Not much older than you, and not nearly as bright."

"Then we're okay. My guess is that whatever you said she didn't understand and whatever she understood won't go any farther. But just in case, if anybody asks or sees you around today, you're our grandfather, just here for a visit to see us for the day. Okay?"

"Makes sense. Makes good sense. You always seem to have yourself a plan, don't you, granddaughter?"

"Great honour, pleasure to meet," Vladimir said as he pumped Mr. McCurdy's arm.

"Mighty fine to meet you, too, son."

"Big girl Sarah and Nicki say many fine things about you."

"I could say some mighty fine things about them, too. Now tell me more about what's happening here."

"What happening is new boss is greedy pig! He nothing but disgusting no good—"

"He's a terrible man," I said, both confirming what Vladimir had started and cutting him off before he got too carried away. "When old Mr. Armstrong died, there was a term in his will that made it impossible for his son to sell the park for three years," I started to say. I had been so relieved when Vladimir said I could explain everything to everybody. "Instead he's selling off the animals bit by bit."

"And the bit he wants to sell now is his tiger," Nick said.

"Kushna is name of tiger," Vladimir said. "Good tiger, nice tiger, old tiger."

"Old or not, there's people who'll pay lots of money—" Mr. McCurdy began.

"Sixty-five thousand dollars," I said, jumping in.

Mr. McCurdy nodded. "I've heard of more being offered. Have to admit that for that kind of money there's lots of people, good people, who'd have their heads turned."

"Boss, not good people. Boss is pig! Disgusting, greedy pig who would sell own mother if—"

"Okay, okay," Mr. McCurdy said, holding up his hands. "I get the idea. The man is a pig."

"Disgusting pig," Vladimir said, almost spitting the words out.

"Right, a disgusting pig. Now how do you even know about this plan to sell off Kushna?"

"I heard him talking to a man," I said.

"Is it possible you heard wrong?" Mr. McCurdy asked.

"Anything's possible, but I was pretty close when it happened."

"How close?"

"As close as Nick is to me right now," I said, pointing to my brother at the other end of the cabin.

"And they talked about their plan with you right there?" Mr. McCurdy questioned.

"They didn't see me. I was hiding. It was the middle of the night, so it was dark."

"Good thing you're telling me about this instead of your mother. She never is too happy about you wandering around in the middle of the night," Mr. McCurdy said with a smirk. "You're sure they didn't know you were there?"

"Positive."

"Good, because this all could be mighty dangerous."

"What do you mean?" Samantha asked.

She'd been surprisingly quiet since Mr. McCurdy and Calvin

had arrived. She'd been keeping a close eye on Calvin who was sitting on my bed, sipping from a can of Coke. If I'd known a chimpanzee would have kept her quiet, I would have tried to get one a few days earlier. When she first walked in, she bumped into Calvin, screamed, and scaled the bunk bed as if it were a tree.

"Well, we're talking a whole lot of money here. People are sometimes willing to do mighty desperate and bad things when money is involved," Mr. McCurdy said.

"Desperate, like what?" I asked.

"'Specially if it might mean going to jail if they're caught."

"They could go to jail for this?" Nick asked.

"The laws on endangered animals are mighty strict. Big fines and the potential for going to jail."

"So we should call the police then," I said. Now I wasn't just worried about Kushna. I was worried about the rest of us.

"Yeah, let's call in the cops and they can arrest them all!" Nick said enthusiastically.

"Not that simple. First, you've got no proof except for Sarah's hearing 'em talk, and second, who you going to call?"

"That was sort of why we called *you* in the first place," I said. "We thought you'd know."

"I do know. It just won't do any good."

"Why not?"

"If we were in India, or other parts of Asia, even Siberia, you'd just call in the local police department, and they'd enforce it."

"But can not do here, right?" Vladimir asked.

"Nope. Local police don't know what to do. Sarah and Nick have already seen that the local police don't know anything about these animals or the laws," he said, referring to the recapture of Buddha when he escaped last summer.

"Maybe they do," Samantha said. "Maybe we should just call and talk to them about it."

"And then they come here and talk to Mr. Armstrong, he denies everything, and they go away," I said. "Then he knows that somebody knows," I said.

"That not good," Vladimir said.

"Not good at all," I agreed. "All we'll do is delay things, maybe a few days or a week, and the next time he'll do it more carefully."

"If only we had some evidence for the police," Nick said.

"Evidence—wait, maybe there is a way to get some evidence," I said.

Chapter 13

"Hello, is this Mrs. Armstrong?" I asked, making my voice sound deeper and older.

"Yes, it is," she said on the other end of the line.

"I'm calling from Granville's Department Store." From all the bags I'd carried in, I knew she did a lot of business with that store.

"Granville's?"

"Yes. We have a package for you."

"A package. I don't know anything about a package. What is it?"

"I don't know, ma'am. It's a box. All wrapped up. Very fancy. And it has your name and address and phone number on it."

"I have no idea what it could be," she said.

"Neither do we, ma'am. I believe it's been here for a long time. Is it possible you requested something that wasn't available and we ordered it in for you? Perhaps you simply forgot?"

"I guess I could have. I was planning on coming into town tomorrow so I'll drop in and—"

"Tomorrow!" I exclaimed, my voice rising to its natural tone. Tomorrow might be too late. I needed them to leave right now. "This evening would be better. You see...it's been undelivered for a while now. Our records show it's been close to two months, and today is the last day before it's no longer available for pickup."

"You're telling me that if I don't pick it up today, then I can't pick it up?"

"Um, yes, exactly."

"And nobody has even attempted to call me before today?"

"No...no, I don't see anything written down," I said.

"Do you have any idea who I am?" she asked angrily.

"You're Mrs. Armstrong," I answered, realizing I must have sounded as confused as she seemed angry.

"I am one of your *best* customers, and this is how I'm being treated. What's your name?" she demanded.

For a second I was so shocked I almost blurted out my real name. "My name is Jane...Jane Smith."

"Well, Jane Smith, you can be certain I'm going to speak to your manager and inform him how poorly this has been handled and what a rude employee he has!"

Rude! The only rude person on this line was her. I had a good mind to...I couldn't do that. "I'm so sorry, Mrs. Armstrong. I really am. It isn't my fault, honestly! I just started working here, and I really need this job. I saw this package, and it's just so beautiful and fancy and pretty, and I knew I had to call."

"Well...maybe this time I won't tell him." She paused, and I could tell she was smirking, enjoying making me squirm. "Is there a bill to be paid on this package?"

"No, ma'am, no bill. All you have to do is come and get it...if you could."

"I imagine I might be able to find time. Tell you what, I'll do you a favour and come and get it right now."

"By yourself?" I needed her husband to leave the house, too. "It's a big package, a really big package, and it'll take more than one person to move it to your vehicle."

"And why can't somebody there help me?" she demanded.

"I guess we could try, but I'm not very big, and it's a very heavy package. I tried to move it and I was afraid I might drop it."

She sighed heavily. "Very well. I'll be there shortly, and I'll bring my husband along, but I want to tell you that he won't be happy about this, not one bit. Is your manager, Mr. Hartley, still there? I'd like to talk to him."

What was I going to do now?

"Is he there?" she asked again.

"I'll check."

I moved the cell phone away from my face, pressing my other hand tightly against the receiver so she couldn't hear anything.

"She wants to speak to the manager!" I whispered.

"Why does she want to do that?" Mr. McCurdy asked.

"To complain."

"Boss wife always complain," Vladimir said. "Nothing ever right with that woman.

"But what do I do?"

"I could pretend to be the manager," Mr. McCurdy said.

"No good. I think she knows him, so she'll know you're not him."

"Just say he's not there right now," Nick said. "Tell her that he's stepped out for a while, but he'll be back when she gets there."

"That's good," I said, nodding. "Fast thinking."

"Thanks, but not nearly as fast as you," he said. "Have you been listening to yourself? You've been great."

Nick complimenting me was perhaps the biggest shock of the whole week, but come to think of it, I had been pretty good.

I brought the phone back up to my face. "I'm sorry, Mrs. Armstrong, but he's not in right now. He stepped out for a minute, but he'll be back by the time you get here. I'll take care of all the paperwork so you can just drop right in and get it. Thank you."

"Yes. I'll see you shortly," she said, and the line went dead.

"That was great, Sarah, just great," Mr. McCurdy said.

"Big girl Sarah very tricky," Vladimir agreed.

"So what do we do now?" Samantha asked.

"We wait," I said. "As soon as they leave, we all get moving."

"That's right," Mr. McCurdy said. "Vladimir and I are going to go over and check on Kushna. I want to have a chance to examine him, and I can't risk that while they're still around the park. It would be hard to explain if they saw me with him after hours."

"We go in cage if want," Vladimir said.

"I do. Can't tell much about a tiger from the outside."

"I want Samantha and Danny to go outside the front gate," I said. "When you see the Armstrongs returning, you're going to phone and let me know they're back."

"Phone you where?" Samantha asked.

"Why, at the Armstrongs' house, of course. Nick and I are going inside to find some evidence."

"We're going to break in?" Nick exclaimed. "Nobody told me about that part of the plan."

"We won't have to break in, I hope. The back door was open the last time." I paused. "I didn't think you'd object to going into their house."

"I'm not objecting. I just didn't know, that's all. You know, Sarah, you're starting to be scary again. Scary, but cool."

"Hopefully we won't have to wait too long before—"

No sooner had I spoken than Mr. and Mrs. Armstrong came out the front door. He didn't look very happy, and she was practically dragging him by the arm. We all ducked so we were completely hidden by the bushes. I shifted around to find a little spot where I could see between the branches. I couldn't pick them out, but then I heard two car doors close, the engine jump to life, and the sound of tires against gravel. The engine roared, and the car raced away, leaving behind a spray of gravel.

"How much time do we have?" I asked.

"Depend on speed. Take Vladimir twenty minutes each way in van."

"Does that include the time it takes to start it and push when it stalls?" Nick asked.

Vladimir smiled. "Big fancy car move faster. Maybe thirty minutes for trip, and ten minutes in store to argue with people. Maybe longer. Boss lady like to argue. We all better go."

⚬

I turned the knob and opened the kitchen door. Thank goodness it was open. We walked into the kitchen. The light over the table was on, and the dishwasher was humming, the little red light glowing at me.

"That was lucky," Nick said. "What were you going to do if the door wasn't open?"

"Keep your voice down," I warned him

"Why? There's nobody here to hear us."

"I know. I just think that..."

Nick smirked.

"Oh, shut up!"

"I didn't say a word," Nick said. "Where do we start?"

"I was thinking his office."

"Good plan. I was hoping to go in there. I thought we could turn on the big-screen TV while we're searching."

"Don't even think about it," I warned.

We quickly moved down the hall to the closed door of the office. I heard a voice coming through the door, and for a split second I panicked. Then I heard a second voice, and a third. It was the TV. I opened the door. The TV was on and blasting. There was a baseball game on.

"I guess I do get to watch TV," Nick said.

"You can listen to it, but I need you to have your eyes looking elsewhere. Don't forget what we're here for, and that we don't have much time." I walked over to the TV and turned the volume way down.

"I thought you said I could listen to it."

"You still can. Just keep your head focused on why we're here."

"I'll remember."

"Let's start with the desk."

"What exactly are we looking for again?" Nick asked.

"I'm not exactly sure. Something to do with the sale of the tiger. Maybe a receipt, or a bill of sale, or a letter—"

"Or an e-mail?" Nick asked.

"Sure, an e-mail, whatever."

"He was on that computer the first time we met him," Nick said.

"And he told me he was going back to search for a buyer for the fawns on the Net. You keep checking the desk. I'll check out the computer."

I moved over and took a seat in front of the computer. When I tapped on the keyboard, the screen lit up—it had been on standby. That was lucky. I recognized the program. It was the same one that was on my computer at home, as well as on all the computers at school. Quickly I scrolled up with the mouse, looking for the e-mail program. I flashed through the various programs until I found it. Then I clicked, and it came up on the screen. "Okay, this is good...very good," I mumbled to myself.

"Did you find something?" Nick asked.

"Nothing we can use, but I can access all his messages by just—" I clicked the mouse "—doing that." The in-box opened, and there were a slew of messages. "I'll start looking. You having any luck?"

"What?" he asked.

"Luck? Have you found anything?"

"Not yet, but my team is up by three runs," he said, pointing at the screen.

I shot him a dirty look. "Keep searching...or else."

I started to open the messages. The first two were just junk mail. I'd gotten that sort of thing on my computer. One offered a way to earn "thousands of dollars a month from the comfort of your home," while the second said it could make me "irresistible to women"—just what I wanted. I opened the next. It was a business letter from somebody who was...

"I've got it!" I almost screamed.

"Let me see," Nick said as he abandoned the search of the desk and crowded in over my shoulder.

I scrolled down the letter. It was from a man named Emanuel, and it sounded as if he was the guy who had been here the night before, the guy who wanted to buy and butcher Kushna.

"The e-mail refers to things, but doesn't discuss them in much detail other than it being a sale," I said. "It's like walking in partway through a conversation."

"Look at the e-mail address and then look back through the in-box to see what else he's sent in other e-mails," Nick suggested.

I minimized the letter, and the in-box jumped back onto the screen. When I scrolled up, there was another letter from that address, and another, and another, and another. Every third e-mail seemed to be from this Emanuel guy. I kept scrolling up. It just went on and on.

"I can't check these all out. There isn't time."

"We don't have to check them all right now," Nick said. "Just print them. We can read them later, and if they say the things we need, we've got a copy in black and white."

"That's smart."

"What can I say?" Nick asked.

"Hopefully nothing for a change. Turn on the printer."

Nick reached over and flicked the switch on the side of the machine. It burped, clicked, whirred, and then came to life.

"I'm going to start with the most recent e-mail and work my way backward," I said.

I hit the print icon, and the first e-mail was sent to the printer. Without delay I called up the next e-mail and printed it, as well.

"Don't forget about the out-box," Nick said. "You need to get his replies to hear both ends."

"I was planning on doing that. How about you stop looking over my shoulder and go back to the desk?"

Nick shrugged and returned to search the desk.

"I'm going to do the last ten e-mails from both the in- and out-boxes that Mr. Armstrong exchanged with this Emanuel guy."

"That sounds good. Assuming we have enough time."

I looked at my watch. It had been almost twenty-five minutes since the Armstrongs had raced away. We still had at least fifteen more minutes before they returned. I just had to keep the e-mails spitting out of the printer, and we'd be long gone before they returned.

"I have to hand it to you, Sarah," Nick said.

I gave him a questioning look.

"You've handled all this fantastically."

I waited for the insult that was sure to follow. "And?" I asked, wanting him to get it over with.

"And what?" he asked.

"Aren't you going to finish that sentence with an insult?"

"Nope. Nothing more to say. You've been really good...of course really bossy, too, like always, but this time you've always had a plan, so I didn't even mind being bossed around that much."

"Thanks...I think."

Suddenly the phone sitting by my elbow rang. I almost jumped out of my chair.

"They're back!" Nick said as headed for the door.

I grabbed the phone. "Are they back?"

There was a long, painful pause that probably lasted about one second.

"Who is this?" a man's voice asked.

Oh, my goodness, it wasn't Samantha.

"Who is this?" he repeated.

"Who is this?" I asked, repeating his question, which seemed like a good one.

He didn't immediately answer, then he said, "This is Emanuel."

I practically dropped the phone.

"And I wish to speak to Mr. Armstrong."

"Armstrong...nope...nobody here by that name."

"Is this not eight, two, zero, eight—"

"Wrong number!" I said, slamming the receiver down.

"We have to get out of here right now!" Nick pleaded. He was standing at the doorway, half of his body out of the room.

"I know we do, but we have to get the last e-mails off the printer. I've already sent them and they're printing. We can't just walk away and leave them. We have to make it look as if nobody's been here. As soon as the last letter prints, I'll shut down the system and turn off the printer, and you make sure things are back in the desk—" I stopped, shocked at what I saw. The entire top of the desk was covered with things Nick had pulled out of the drawers in his search.

The phone rang again, and I screamed.

"We have to go!" Nick shouted.

"We can't until we put things back, or they'll know somebody was here."

"But the phone!" Nick protested.

"I won't answer it this time."

"But what if it's Samantha warning us they're back?"

I hadn't thought of that. "It's probably just that man. Wouldn't you call right back if you'd dialled a wrong number?"

"But it could be Samantha."

"Even if it is, we still have two minutes until they get to the house. That's enough time."

The phone kept ringing. Each ring seemed louder and more piercing.

"Just put everything back into the drawers."

"I don't know where it all goes," Nick said frantically. "I can't remember."

"Just try. I'll help you as soon as I close down the computer."

"I don't even know why he keeps most of that stuff. It's just a lot of trash and—"

"Trash?" I questioned, cutting him off.

"Yeah, garbage."

"That's it, trash. I have to check the trash."

"Sarah, we don't have time to search the garbage cans now! We have to leave!"

Nick sounded as if he was close to tears.

"Not the garbage cans. The trash on the e-mail. If you were doing something that you didn't want Mom to see, wouldn't you trash it?"

"I guess so."

The phone had stopped ringing. "It must have been that guy," I said. "If it was Samantha, she would have let it ring until we got it. Now finish up with the desk."

Nick remained frozen in place.

"Look, Nick, I'm not leaving until it's all put away. You can stand there until the Armstrongs come back, or you can help."

He took a tentative, hesitant step back toward the desk.

"Hurry!" I barked, and he jumped back into full speed.

I clicked on the trash bin. There was only one e-mail. I was just about to open it when I heard the sound of a car. I looked up at Nick. The expression on his face left no doubt he'd heard it, too, and his heart had also jumped into his throat.

"Just finish up!" I practically yelled.

I clicked on the print button. Whatever that trashed message was would print. Nick started to sweep things off the desk and into drawers. That certainly couldn't be exactly where he had found them, but anything was better than stuff sitting on top.

"Come on, come on," I said to the printer, encouraging it to print faster.

"I'm done," Nick said.

"It's almost finished printing. Turn the TV back up."

The printer spit out the page. I pushed the off button at the same second Nick turned up the volume on the TV—it felt as if the two were somehow connected. I grabbed the sheet out of the printer tray and...the computer...I didn't have time to shut it down properly. So I just pushed the power button, and the screen faded away.

"Come on, we'll go out the back door."

We raced out of the room. The door was open. I skidded to a stop and went back to close it.

"Hurry, Sarah!" Nick hissed.

I bounded after him and into the kitchen. We'd head out the back door just as they were coming in the front. The kitchen door opened. With the last pulse of blood through my heart before it stopped beating completely, I grabbed Nick and we dropped behind the kitchen table.

"It isn't my fault!" Mrs. Armstrong protested as she walked through the doorway.

"Who's fault do you think it is then?" her husband asked as he followed her and slammed the door behind him.

"That stupid store and that horrid woman who called me."

Look who was talking! Nick and I slid forward so that we were better hidden under the tablecloth, which hung down almost to the floor.

"Are you sure you got the name of the store right?" he demanded. "The sign on the door at Granville's said it had been closed for two hours."

"I know my stores."

"That you certainly do. You know every store in the entire town."

"Are you saying I shop too much?"

"If the shoe fits, buy it seems to be your motto."

"Well, I never!" she huffed.

"Never what? Certainly never didn't buy it? Have you ever met a shoe you didn't like? Do you have any idea how many pairs of shoes you own?"

"I don't count them, I wear them so—"

"One hundred and eighty-three pairs!"

"You've been counting my shoes?" she shrieked.

"There are some small countries where the whole population doesn't own one hundred and eighty-three pairs of shoes between them!"

"I'm so glad you can count!" she snapped. "Do you know how many bedrooms this house has?"

"Well...three, of course."

"Perfect number. One for me, one for you, and one sitting empty between us. Good night!"

I heard her stomp out of the room.

"Honey, come on. I didn't mean anything!"

I peeked out from under the table and saw his feet disappear down the hall. "Come on, now's our chance."

I started to stand up just as the phone rang. I had to stifle the urge to cry out. It rang out a second time, and I head somebody coming back toward us. I dropped back to the floor.

"I'm coming...I'm coming!" Mr. Armstrong called out as he returned. "Hello!" he barked.

There was silence as he listened for the response.

"I didn't expect to hear from you tonight."

I wondered if it was that Emanuel guy calling back again.

"No, we just got in. We had to pick up something at a store. At least I thought we were supposed to pick something up."

Again he listened for a reply. I shifted slightly so I could see his feet.

"No, we just got back...no...nobody."

Emanuel was asking about the call—the "wrong" number.

"Look, can I call you back later? I have something I have to take care of."

Again he listened and, of course, I couldn't hear.

"I know it's a lot of money. Hold on and let me take this in my office where I have my notes."

I hoped his notes weren't in his desk, or he'd instantly be suspicious. I watched his feet retreat out of the room once again until they disappeared down the hall.

"Now!" I whispered, getting to my feet and heading for the door.

Nick followed, still on all fours, crawling as fast as he could across the floor. I pulled open the door, and Nick crawled straight through and out into the night. I followed, closing the door behind me. Up ahead I saw Nick. He'd finally risen to his feet and plunged into the cover of the trees. I doubled my pace and hit the same gap only a few seconds later, skidding to a stop and almost crashing into Nick. He'd stopped a few feet into the cover and had dropped to his knees again.

"Are you all right?" I panted.

"Fine...good...now."

"That was close," I said, working to catch my breath, as well.

"It couldn't have been any closer. Let's get to Vladimir's so we can look at the e-mails."

I was still clutching them tightly in my hands. Either I had the proof we needed, or simply a bunch of crunched-up pieces of paper.

Nick and I sat at the kitchen table. Nobody was back yet. I spread the e-mails out on the table in front of me, attempting to straighten them out. "Let's try to get them in order and then—"

The door burst open, and Samantha and Danny came into the room.

"We were so worried when you didn't answer the phone, but then we figured you'd already gotten out," Samantha said.

"We were still there when it rang," I said.

"You were?" Danny asked.

"Heck, we were still there when they drove up," I said.

"And when they walked in the house," Nick added.

"You were still in the house?" Samantha gasped.

I nodded. The look of shock on Samantha's and Danny's faces was almost worth what we'd gone through.

"Did you...did you find anything?" Samantha asked.

"We don't know yet. We have to look through these," I said, pointing at the e-mails spread out in front of us. "We'll just put them in order, organize them, and carefully sort through them—"

"Here it is!" Nick said, holding up one of the e-mails. "It's all right here!"

"What's right there?"

"The final price of the tiger—sixty-five thousand dollars— what they're going to do with it and where they're going to do it. All we need to prove everything is right here!"

I ripped the paper out of his hands and studied it. He was right. Everything we needed was all there.

"Now that we have the proof, all we need is to tell some- body who can do something about it."

🐾

"I don't even know why we have to watch Kushna tonight," Nick said. "It's all right in the e-mail, just like you overheard, and it's not happening until tomorrow night."

"We're going to do it because that's the plan," I explained. "Remember how much you admired my good planning?"

"But it's cold and I don't want to go out."

"Come on, Nick, don't be such a whiner. You're only going out for two hours, and you're not going to be alone."

He and Danny were going out from ten until midnight. Then Samantha and I would follow until two in the morning. Mr. McCurdy and Calvin would replace us for two more hours, and then Vladimir would be in charge until daybreak.

"You don't see Calvin complaining, do you?" I asked.

Calvin looked at us, raised his eyebrows, and then let loose a thunderous burp.

"I think he does that on purpose," Nick said.

"I think he's had too much Coke to drink," I suggested.

"Blame Vladimir. He's given him at least a half dozen. He doesn't seem to be able to say no to him."

"He is kind of cute," Samantha said.

"That's not what you thought the first time you saw him," I said, chuckling as I pictured her jumping straight into the top bunk bed.

"He surprised me, that's all," she said defensively. She walked over and sat beside Calvin. He reached out, pulled her to him, and planted a big kiss on her cheek.

Everybody burst into laughter, and Calvin let out a shriek of delight that caused Samantha to jump to her feet.

"I think he likes you," Nick said.

"And I'd like *you* to get going," I said. "Go and get warmly dressed, and I'll make up a thermos of hot chocolate for you two to drink while you're there.

For tonight we were all bunking down in Vladimir's place. There were two bedrooms—his and one for Mr. McCurdy to use—and we'd taken the mattresses from our cabin and placed them on the floor of the living room. At first I wasn't sure why we were doing all of this, but somehow it seemed safer to be in one place.

Although we'd lain down over an hour ago, I hadn't been able to sleep. I'd hoped to grab an hour or so of shut-eye before having to go out and replace the boys, but it was useless. It wasn't just the tension and excitement about what was going on, but the loud voices in the other room. I didn't think that either Mr. McCurdy or Vladimir knew how to be quiet. With Vladimir it was because he was just so huge that he needed a huge voice to go along with him. With Mr. McCurdy it had more to do with his hearing. I'd noticed over the past year that as his hearing had gotten a bit worse, his voice had gotten louder. And now on the phone it seemed especially loud. And that was what the two of them were doing. They were on the phone, Samantha's cell phone, making calls, trying desperately to locate the proper authorities. Now that we had the proof, we needed to find the right people to present it to.

"You still awake, Sarah?" Samantha asked.

"Yep. Did you sleep at all?" I asked her.

She shook her head. "Not a wink. Boy, those guys are loud."

"I wouldn't mind if they were loud if I thought they had gotten hold of somebody."

"Yeah, I don't think they got the right person," Samantha agreed. "Since I'm not going to get to sleep, anyway, I'm going to get up."

"Me, too."

We slowly got up, stretched, and headed for the kitchen, entering in the middle of a telephone conversation.

"So let me get this straight," Mr. McCurdy barked into the phone. "You agree that it's illegal to kill tigers because they're endangered, and your whole organization is dedicated to saving them, but you can't help me unless the tiger's in a jungle. Is that what you're saying?"

There was silence as the person on the other end responded.

"I only have one other question," Mr. McCurdy said. "Did your parents raise any kids who didn't grow up to be complete idiots?"

"I thought girls try to sleep," Vladimir said as he turned and saw us.

"Tried. No luck," I said.

"Well, I'm having no luck with these calls, either," Mr. McCurdy said. "Everybody and his brother says they want to save the lives of tigers, but they can't do anything unless they're in the wild. They agree that it's illegal to kill one in captivity, but they can't help me stop it. As far as I can figure, there's only one way to save the life of that tiger." He paused and smiled, and we all waited for his answer. "We're just going to have to steal it."

"You can't steal the tiger," Samantha said.

"Course I can," Mr. McCurdy said. "I could put it in my car and drive away."

"You can't put a tiger in a car!" she exclaimed.

"You haven't seen his car," I said. "It's specially build to transport large animals. His tiger, Buddha, goes in there all the time."

"But still, stealing is...wrong."

"Letting the tiger be slaughtered is wrong. Stealing it is right!"

"But if you get caught, you'll get in big trouble."

"Ah, now," Mr. McCurdy said, holding up a finger to make a point, "that's the secret. Don't get caught."

"You can take it home and it can live right on your farm with Buddha," I said. "There's plenty of space. They could be pals and keep each other company."

"But stealing..." Samantha sighed.

"It really wouldn't be like stealing," I said. "Especially if the head zookeeper thought it was right."

We all looked at Vladimir, who had been silent during the discussion.

"Well?" I asked, breaking the silence.

"No steal Kushna," he said quietly.

"But if he doesn't then—"

Vladimir raised his hands and stood up, cutting me off.

"No *steal* tiger...*rescue* tiger. We make plan."

❧

"I still don't know why we can't do it tonight," I said.

"Tomorrow is better," Mr. McCurdy said. "They're not going to take the tiger till dark, so we'll take him some time between the closing of the park and nightfall."

"That's cutting things a bit tight, isn't it?" I asked.

"A bit, but we really haven't got much choice. With a tiger in my trunk I'm going to have to drive straight through, so I need some good sleep tonight. It isn't like Calvin is going to keep me awake talking."

"I have an idea," I said.

"I know what your idea is, and I'm not letting you take my shift tonight," Mr. McCurdy said knowingly.

"That's not what I was going to suggest."

"It isn't?"

I smiled. "I think you should take Nick and me with you."

"You two?"

"Sure. We're supposed to fly out Saturday, anyway, so we'd just be leaving a little early."

"Hmm...the company wouldn't be a bad thing," he agreed. "And I could use the help if anything goes wrong."

"We could get all packed and ready to go. Do you think the Armstrongs would notice if we're gone early and connect that to the tiger being gone?" I asked Vladimir.

"Not notice nothing most days," Vladimir replied. "After tiger go missing, they have other things to worry about."

"What will they think happened to it?"

"They'll think Emanuel came early and stole it from them, is my bet," Mr. McCurdy said.

"So it could be messy when he does show up," Samantha said.

"More than messy, 'cause when he finds the tiger's gone, he'll figure they already sold it to somebody else for more money," Mr. McCurdy said. "There's no honour among thieves, so neither will be able to convince the other that they didn't do it. It'll be one rip-roaring fight for sure. Vladimir, it might be smart for you to take Danny and Samantha away for the evening and have 'em sleep up here in your guest bedroom."

"I take good care. Nobody bother children with Vladimir here," he said, pounding a fist against his chest.

"Won't the Armstrongs just call the police and report it missing?" Samantha asked.

"Report that the tiger they were going to illegally sell and slaughter has gone missing?" Mr. McCurdy said. "It ain't going to happen. And the next day Vladimir will get you to the airport and you'll be home."

"But how will we find out what happened?" Samantha asked. "How will we know everything went all right?"

"We'll give you our phone number," I said. "You can call us the day you get back. Vladimir can call us, too, and tell us what happened here."

"Vladimir can do more than call," Mr. McCurdy said. "As soon as he gets a day or two off, he can come on up and visit."

"Like to visit McCurdy," Vladimir said. "Like much."

"There you go," Mr. McCurdy said. "It's just about the perfect plan. You girls better get down and relieve the boys now or—" He stopped at the sound of feet running up the path.

The door burst open, and Nick came running in. "They've come for the tiger!" he yelled.

Chapter 14

Everybody stood in stunned silence, then Danny came running in a few seconds later. "They're here! The bad men have... come," he panted desperately.

"Are you sure?" I finally asked.

"Am I sure?" Nick questioned. "Of course I'm sure! It's Armstrong and three other men. They have a truck, and behind the truck is a trailer, the sort you use for moving animals!"

"They can't be here for any other reason," Mr. McCurdy said.

"What are we going to do?" Nick demanded.

"I don't know," I muttered, shaking my head.

"Vladimir know," he said, starting for the door. "Only boss and three other men. Vladimir go and beat up all four and throw in back of trailer."

Mr. McCurdy grabbed him by the arm. "Can't let you do that, Vlad. No telling about men like these. Desperate, lots of money at stake, and I'm betting dollars to doughnuts if they're trying to move a tiger at least one of them's carrying some heat."

"Heat?" I asked.

"A gun. At least a tranquillizer gun and maybe something else just in case the tiger gets loose. You're a big guy, Vladimir, but nobody's too big that they can't get shot. We need a plan."

"Have you got one?" Nick asked.

"Well, I have the start of a plan," Mr. McCurdy said.

"The start?" I asked.

"Yep. Vladimir, grab that bottle of vodka from the cupboard over top of the fridge."

Everybody stared as if Mr. McCurdy had lost his mind.

"Do what I told you to!" he yelled, and Vladimir scurried across the room to grab the bottle. If everything hadn't been so serious, it would have been funny to watch this hulk of a man jumping at Mr. McCurdy's words.

"Take a deep swig of vodka," he ordered.

Vladimir twisted off the cap and took a big gulp.

"Now spit it in the sink," Mr. McCurdy said.

Vladimir's look showed complete shock. He spat it out. "Waste of good vodka," he said, shaking his head.

"Not a waste. I need you to smell like you've been drinking. I want you to get down to Kushna's pen and start talking to those men, maybe sing a little song when you wander up. Make 'em think you've been drinking and do whatever you can to slow 'em down. I need them delayed by at least thirty minutes."

"And then?" I asked.

"By then we'll have figured out what to do next."

My mouth dropped open, and everybody else's stunned look mirrored my thoughts.

Mr. McCurdy shrugged. "Unless any of you got an idea right now?"

Nobody answered.

"In that case you better get moving, Vladimir. Slow 'em down." He started for the door.

"And, big guy," Mr. McCurdy called out. Vladimir stopped and turned around. "You just got to slow 'em down, not stop 'em. The last thing we need is a dead Russian hero. Understand?"

Vladimir's face broke into a goofy smile. "Understand, boss."

We watched him leave, the door slamming shut behind him.

"Well, Sarah, so what are we going to do?" Mr. McCurdy asked.

"I...I don't know," I stammered.

"We're going to videotape them," Samantha said. "I can sneak up really close and use my video camera to tape the whole thing."

"That's a great idea!" Mr. McCurdy said.

"Only half a great idea," I disagreed. "That'll give evidence to bring to the authorities, but it won't stop them from driving away with Kushna and killing him."

"I'm still not sure how we can do anything about that," Mr. McCurdy said. "They're going to buy that tiger tonight no matter what we do."

"Unless...unless..." I stopped and smiled. I had it. "Unless somebody else buys it instead."

"Somebody else?" Nick asked.

"Yes. I was thinking that somebody else could come tonight and offer more than sixty-five thousand dollars for the tiger."

"What good would that do?" Nick asked.

"It would do a lot of good." I turned to Mr. McCurdy. "If it's Mr. McCurdy."

"Mr. McCurdy?" Nick asked.

"I haven't got time to explain all this right now," I said. "I'll tell Mr. McCurdy while you three go back to the cabin and get the video camera."

We moved along the path. It was dark, rough, and hard to move, but at least we didn't have to be quiet. From the time we'd gotten even remotely close to Kushna's pen, we could hear Vladimir. At first I was scared when I heard him yelling, but then he started to laugh, and for the past thirty seconds he'd been bellowing out some sort of Russian folk song—loud and tremendously out of key. I had to hand it to him. He did sound drunk. And more than a little bit crazy.

Clearing a stand of bushes, we could easily see the cluster of men standing in front of the tiger's cage and holding flashlights. I could make out five figures as well as the darkened outline of a truck.

"Too late to look at animals!" Vladimir bellowed. "All come back to house for drink! Enough vodka for all!"

"You've had enough to drink for all of us already," Mr. Armstrong stated loudly. He sounded angry.

"Too dark, too late to look at animal."

"Go away and sleep it off!" Mr. Armstrong yelled.

"No want to sleep. Want to sing. Want to dance!"

Vladimir reached over, grabbed one of the men, picked him up off the ground, and started to dance him around.

"Let me go! Let me go! I order you to let me down this minute!"

He was flinging around Mr. Armstrong!

"Sure thing, boss," Vladimir said as he dropped him and he fell to the ground, landing on his bottom. Mr. Armstrong got back to his feet quickly.

I had to stifle a laugh. We were near enough now that they could hear me

"This is close enough," Samantha whispered as she stopped and took shelter behind some bushes. "I can use the zoom from here," she said, her voice barely audible even to me standing right beside her.

Danny and Nick dropped right beside us.

"You guys no fun!" Vladimir yelled. "No want to dance, no want to drink, no want to sing!"

"For the last time I'm ordering you to leave!" Mr. Armstrong bellowed. "If you don't, then I'm going to kick you right off the property! Now leave!"

"Vladimir leave...you no fun."

We watched as Vladimir walked out of the halo of light thrown by the flashlights and was swallowed by the darkness. He continued to sing as he moved, and his voice slowly faded away until finally the only sound was the chirping of crickets.

"What now?" Nick asked in a hushed tone.

"We wait while Samantha videos—are you sure you're close enough?" I asked.

"I thought I was, but now that Vladimir isn't yelling, and they're not yelling back at him, I can't hear them anymore. I can see them okay, but I can't hear what they're saying."

"Then we need to get closer," I whispered. "But not all of us. Danny, Nick, I want you two to go that way, circle around, but stay a good distance away. Samantha, you and I will sneak up until we get close enough to hear them."

"This is going to be really hard," Samantha said. "Are you sure we can't stay here?"

"It's no good if we can't hear so—"

I was stopped by the rumbling sound of a car engine and lights bouncing down the path.

"Is that Mr. McCurdy?" Samantha asked.

"It had better be," I said. I prayed it was him. This plan was shaky enough without anything else unexpected being thrown in.

"Move now," I said to Samantha as I took her by the arm and we quickly moved forward. I figured the noise of Mr. McCurdy's car would hide the sound of our feet, and that every eye would be staring at him hurtling toward them.

Keeping low to the ground, we moved from the cover of one bush to a tree, then to another bush, finally landing behind a thick outcrop no more than five meters away. Suddenly the lights from the car illuminated the cover, blinding us. Panic-stricken, I flattened myself on the ground. The lights passed as the car turned, but for a few seconds I couldn't see anything except the stars bursting in my eyes.

"Which one of you is Armstrong?" I heard Mr. McCurdy's voice call out.

"Start videotaping," I whispered.

"I'm Armstrong, and I don't know who you are or why you're

here, but you have to leave right now!" he ordered.

"Who I am isn't important. Why I'm here is. I want to make you an offer for your tiger."

"My tiger...my tiger isn't for sale," he gasped.

"Sure it is, and this here fella, Emanuel, is buying it."

"How do you know my name?" the little man questioned. He was the man I'd seen before.

"I know lots. Don't get old without knowing things," Mr. McCurdy said. "Things like the price you're paying for a tiger and all the details about where and when and what you're going to be doing."

"Why are you here?" Mr. Armstrong asked. He sounded worried.

"I'm here to make you a rich man. This guy's playing you for a chump. I'm prepared to offer you ninety-three."

"Ninety-three!" Mr. Armstrong gasped.

"That's right. Ninety-three thou—"

"We've got a deal!" Emanuel said. "A deal you're going to hon-our!" He came toward Mr. Armstrong in a threatening manner.

"Honour?" Mr. McCurdy said with a laugh. "Ain't no honour in anything any of us is doing here. This is about money, and I'm offering more right now right up front. Got it in my car."

"Stay out of this, old man, if you know what's good for you."

"I know what's good for me," Mr. McCurdy said. "I know what's good for everybody. And I'll soon see just how smart you all are."

"Smart enough not to come out here by myself," Emanuel said. "There's four of us, old man, and you didn't think that maybe we wouldn't be carrying some protection?" His voice was quiet and scary.

Mr. McCurdy laughed. "That's good thinking. At least it would be good thinking if it wasn't for the fact that all of you are standing right there together in the lights of my car. While my people, and there are *five* of them, are standing all around you in the dark, hidden behind trees...watching."

"You're bluffing." Emanuel said.

"Am I?" Mr. McCurdy questioned. "Time for a little demonstration." He turned and faced away from the men. "I don't want anybody to stand up or reveal their location, but I want you to pick up a rock and throw it toward where these men are standing."

A rock? He wanted us to throw rocks at them?

"Do it," Samantha said.

I grabbed a rock and began to stand up to try to throw it when two rocks came bouncing into the light. One landed at their feet, and the second bounced and hit Mr. Armstrong in the leg, causing him to jump into the air. Awkwardly I threw my rock, trying to stay low. There was a loud, smashing sound. In shock I dropped to the ground.

"You broke the side window of their truck!" Samantha whispered.

"If they can do that with rocks, you got a pretty good idea what they could do with rifles," Mr. McCurdy said. "Now I think it's time we did us a little business. Anybody want to hear what I have in mind?"

Nobody answered, but I knew I wanted to hear.

"I'm gonna make Mr. Armstrong ninety-three thousand dollars richer. Do you want to be ninety-three thousand dollars richer?"

"Sure, of course," Mr. Armstrong said.

"And being rich is better than being in jail."

"What do you mean, jail?"

"Jail time is what you get for killing an endangered animal. You should know that. And I've got enough evidence to put you all away."

"What do you mean, evidence?" Mr. Armstrong asked.

"E-mails, pictures, recorded telephone conversations."

"That was you who was in my house, looking at my e-mail, rummaging through my desk, answering the phone," Mr. Armstrong gasped.

Obviously he'd found out somebody had been there. If only

we'd had a few more minutes to put things back the right way.

"That's why you decided to move a day early," Mr. McCurdy said. "But we knew that, too. Your choice, Armstrong. You can be rich or you can be in jail. Make a decision."

"And what about us?" Emanuel asked, jumping in before he could answer.

"What about you?" Mr. McCurdy asked.

"You don't just expect us to walk away, do you?"

"Nope. I expect you all to put your tails between your legs and run away—fast and far. And if I ever hear about you operating around here, around my territory, everything we have will be forwarded to the people who can put you away for years."

"Are you threatening me?" Emanuel asked.

"Nope. Promising you. Go now while you still can."

There was silence. Everything came down to this moment. What if he didn't believe Mr. McCurdy? What if he wouldn't go? What if they were carrying guns?

"Everybody into the truck," he said, and the three men moved toward the vehicle. They climbed in and the doors slammed shut. Emanuel hadn't moved. "I'm not going to forget you," he snarled at Mr. McCurdy as he moved toward him.

"And I won't forget you. If ever I'm thinking my memory is failing, I'll just look at my pictures or listen to the tapes to help remind me. Get out now!" Mr. McCurdy barked as he stepped even closer to the man.

Emanuel hurried over to the truck. Its engine started and the lights came on. Before it could start moving Mr. McCurdy walked directly in front of the vehicle and held his arms up. "My men will be watching you the whole way out!" he yelled. "Don't stop, don't slow down, and don't even think about coming back!" he yelled, stepping out of the way.

The truck's engine roared and it started off. I watched it move up the path, keeping my eyes on it until it reached the top of the path and dropped over the ridge. I could still hear the engine, getting quieter and quieter until it faded away completely. Now not even the crickets were chirping. It was almost as if they were waiting for what would come next, too.

"So, you said you have the money with you?" Mr. Armstrong asked, finally breaking the silence.

Mr. McCurdy laughed. "I've got everything you're going to need. Let's just make sure we both understand what's going to happen."

"Sure."

"You're selling me your tiger, Kushna."

"That's right."

"And I'm paying you ninety-three thousand dollars."

"Most generous," Mr. Armstrong said.

"And you know what I'm going to do with the tiger, right?"

"Of course."

"Explain it to me. I want to hear you."

Mr. Armstrong hesitated. "Well, you're going to...going to... dispose of it."

"Dispose is such a polite word. You know that I'm going to slaughter it, right?"

"Yes, of course."

"And then butcher it, remove the organs, and grind down the bones to make herbal remedies."

"Yes, I understand," Mr. Armstrong said.

"And that doesn't bother you?"

"It's just an animal."

"That's where you're wrong," Mr. McCurdy said. "A cow is an animal. This isn't just an animal. This is a tiger. An endangered animal. One of only a few thousand left anywhere in the entire world, and you're going to profit from its slaughter."

"Not just me. You're making a profit, too," Mr. Armstrong said.

"Believe me, I'm going to be making a good profit on this," Mr. McCurdy said. "Vladimir, are you somewhere you can hear me?"

"Here!" Vladimir's voice came booming out of the darkness

and his darkened silhouette appeared. He walked into the light and stopped beside Mr. McCurdy.

"You...you...know Vladimir?" Mr. Armstrong stammered. There was enough light for me to see a look of complete confusion on his face.

"Told you I know lots of things. I also know I'm changing the deal."

"What do you mean?" Mr. Armstrong questioned.

"I'm not buying the tiger off you because you don't own it."

"Of course I own it!" he thundered.

"Nope, you don't own the tiger, or that lion over there, or the deer. Nothing."

"You're insane! Everything here belongs to me."

"*Did* belong to you," Mr. McCurdy said.

"You get off my land right now, or I'll call the police!" he threatened.

"Good, that would save me making the phone call myself." Mr. McCurdy paused. "I want to show them the e-mails you and Emanuel were writing and, of course, the videotape. Sarah, Samantha, Danny, Nick, come on down here."

We slowly got up. Samantha still had her eye to the viewfinder and kept taping as we walked toward them. Nick and Danny came from the opposite direction.

"You still taping, Samantha?" Mr. McCurdy asked.

"Yep. I got it all. Everything."

"Give me that tape!" Mr. Armstrong yelled. He took a couple of steps toward us, and I felt my heart race.

"You want arm ripped right off?" Vladimir asked, grabbing Mr. Armstrong, spinning him around, and picking him right up off the ground

"Let go of me!" Mr. Armstrong pleaded. "Let me go!"

"You not boss of Vladimir anymore!" the big Russian yelled.

"It's okay," Mr. McCurdy said. "Put him down. There's no need to break anything...if you don't have to."

Vladimir released his hold, and Mr. Armstrong dropped to the ground.

"Here's the new deal I got for you," Mr. McCurdy said. "You walk up to that fancy house of yours, take whatever you can stuff in your vehicle, and you and your wife leave."

"Leave? What do you mean leave?"

"Drive away and don't come back."

"I can't do that," Mr. Armstrong pleaded. "If I leave, I'll lose everything—the house, the park, all the animals."

"You've already lost everything. I'm giving you a chance to get something," Mr. McCurdy said.

"What will I get?" he asked.

"Your freedom. If you leave now, I keep the tape and you'll stay out of jail. Stay, and I turn the tape over. You'll go to jail and you'll still lose everything. I'm only giving you this chance out of respect for your father."

"You knew my father?"

"Sure enough did. Fine animal man he was."

"But...but...this isn't fair," Mr. Armstrong stammered.

"Sounds pretty fair to me. Stay, and go to jail and lose everything. Or just leave and lose everything. What's it going to be?"

"I'm going to...I'm going to leave," he said, his voice barely a whisper.

"Good choice!" Mr. McCurdy exclaimed, slapping him on the back.

"Vladimir and I are going to be spending the night right up there at the main gate making sure that once you leave, you stay gone."

Mr. Armstrong stood there, silent, unmoving. Everybody watched and waited.

"If you need some help in getting started, I'm mighty sure Vladimir would be more than willing to lend you a hand...or an arm...or a fist."

Vladimir chuckled ominously, and Mr. Armstrong staggered

up the path.

"We won," I said quietly, my voice shaking with emotion. "We won."

"No," Vladimir said, shaking his head. "Not win. Everybody lose."

"What do you mean?" I asked. "Kushna's safe, Mr. Armstrong has to leave so the land becomes a park, and you...you get all the animals!"

"Vladimir own animals, but not own place to keep. Not even have place to keep Vladimir. All must go. Not just Kushna, but all animals. All are lost," he said sadly.

"I'm so sorry," I said. I just hadn't thought it through. What good was owning all the animals if you didn't have any place to keep them? Poor animals. Poor Vladimir. He'd have to sell off or give up all the animals and—I stopped myself.

"Mr. McCurdy," I said. "I was wondering. How many acres is your farm?"

"It's about two hundred acres and—" He stopped and turned to Vladimir. "How'd you and Kushna and all the animals like to come for a visit...stay a while...as long as you need?"

"You mean, you mean?" Vladimir stammered.

Mr. McCurdy smiled. "Sarah, Nicholas, meet your new neighbour."